BLOOD OF THE DEVOTED

BLOOD OF THE DEVOTED

STACIE TURNER

TEALSTONE
WRENSAW
SILVERBONE MOUNTAINS
RIVER URSA
HARETHORN
BELLHOPE
YAMMOOR
WALNUT WOODS
BYRNE
EASTERN HILLS
SCHLAFHOLD
HAUNTED LAKE
SOUTHERN FOREST

Content warning:
This book contains explicit steamy romance scenes intended
for an adult audience. Reader discretion is advised.

CHAPTER 1

The smell of fresh bread engulfs my senses until I'm practically drunk on the aroma. A daily occurrence when one works in a bakery. Then there's the warmth from the oven, like a gentle embrace. Dad slaps another lump of dough on the counter, a sound as familiar as my rumbling stomach. Flour coats my fingertips. All of these things sing of home. The only life I know.

I pull out a fresh set of loaves on a tray. The edges are browned to perfection. I inhale the crispness.

"You know, I'm kind of hoping we don't get any customers today," I say, "If it means we get to finish the leftovers."

Dad rolls his eyes. To him, bread is just bread. It's his work.

Of course, my wish for no customers is quickly denied. As per usual, the regulars come streaming into the bakery as soon as we open. Actually, ten minutes before we open. There's no stopping them.

First is always Prudence, clutching at her burlap sack which still contains crumbs from the previous day. For all she talks, she has never mentioned her family to me. I assume she has children or grandchildren given that she goes through a whole loaf on the daily. I would struggle with that, even with my love of bread.

"Ah, Minnow, lovely to see you, as always," Prudence says, pulling me into a hug over the counter and pecking me on the cheek. I ignore the pain of the edge of the bench digging into my abdomen.

"Perry, what have you concocted for us all this morning?" she addresses Dad.

"Just the usual," Dad replies. Then, after a pause, he pulls out a few loaves wrapped in paper. "Plus these... fig and poppy seed. The fruits were a kind donation from Ms Creed. Would you like one, Prudence? First customer of the day gets it half-price."

Prudence swats her hand to the side dismissively. "No, you know I don't believe in fruit-bread. No need to go mixing things that each do better on their own." She hands some coins over to Dad, who places a brown loaf in her sack.

Next through the door is Sal. I've known her all twenty-two years of my life, but she looks as young as when I first saw her. People say that she did a Witch a favour once when she was twenty-eight, and since then she's been Blessed with endless youth. Or at least the visage of it. I'm not sure I see the appeal. Why would you want everyone to treat you like you were young when you've got so much life experience and wisdom to offer? And surely love would be painful – loving those your age but never looking like someone they should love? My theory is the Witch tricked her into wishing for something she didn't understand the consequences of. Witches aren't known for their honesty and goodwill.

I've only encountered one Witch. I was about nine. The whole village went quiet as she passed through, bolting their doors and guiding their children away from the windows.

I had been working at the bakery, and Dad was sick in bed. It didn't occur to me that anything was amiss that day: the sun still shone and the bread smelled as good as ever. I was wrapping a round loaf into a paper parcel when I saw her out the window: a hunched figure wearing a midnight blue veil which hid her face as she slowly ambled down the street. Around her wrist she wore a circle of river reeds woven together.

I couldn't understand why I felt a sudden chill in my chest, as if my heart was frosting over. Despite the discomfort, I brushed the flour off my hands and went to the door, which always hung ajar to welcome customers.

I stood in the doorway just as she passed. Even though she was in the middle of the street, it felt as if she was only an arm's length away. The eeriness of the surroundings began to sink in, and I realised everyone else had vanished. This woman – could she even be called a woman? – and I were the only souls in sight. The curiosity within me was drowned out by the terror I felt. It was the feeling that I'd stepped into a room and seen something that I shouldn't have.

Just as I began to back away from the doorway, the Witch turned in my direction. Even though her eyes were covered by the veil, I could tell she was looking directly at me.

For some reason, rather than grabbing the door handle with my quivering hand and staggering inside, I stayed there and held her gaze. Chest puffed out, palms closed, jaw clenched.

A moment passed, and then she turned and continued on her way.

I never told my parents about what had happened. When Dad asked me if I had seen the Witch everyone was talking about, I said I had been throwing out burnt bread. I felt like I had to keep a secret and that the Witch would know it if I hadn't.

Sal shows more interest in the fig and poppy seed bread. She's clearly more adventurous than Prudence. Sal flashes Dad a smile on the way out, showing off her sharp canine teeth. Sometimes I wonder if she's flirting with him. Dad has mentioned knowing her when they were children, so maybe she's his age. It's hard to imagine, comparing her to my Dad with his thin grey hair, lined forehead, spotted hands and crow's feet.

A few more customers wander in, happy to purchase their bread with a quick "please" and "thank you" before heading on their way. Others stop to chat, commenting on the weather or the new bridge. Everyone is ecstatic about the new bridge. The River Ursa passes by the edge of the village, and for almost a year the bridge to the eastern side has been uncrossable due to storm damage. People had to travel five hours north through the forest on foot to reach the next crossing. The newly-erected bridge has been a hot talking topic for over a week now.

I've grown a bit weary of the conversation myself, but old Betty Gray has a contagious enthusiasm that draws me in today.

"A bunch of lads are heading out to Haunted Lake for a day of fishing," she says cheerily. "Now they can march straight across and follow the eastern path."

"No-one should be visiting somewhere called 'Haunted Lake'," says Dad with a shake of his head.

Betty swats his arm. "Oh, please. You used to head out there every weekend when you were in school. Your lot hauled boats along and everything."

Dad shrugs. "Maybe we shouldn't have. There are eels in that water, you know. And it's murkier than muddy puddles."

"Can I go?" I ask, turning to Dad.

"Don't see why you'd want to," murmurs Dad.

We both suddenly remember that I'm well and truly an adult and can go wherever I please. It's easy to forget, since our relationship and daily life haven't changed for the past fourteen years since I started working at the bakery.

"You can do what you like in your own time," Dad states. "But your shift lasts another three hours."

I sigh.

Betty glances at me with a sparkle in her eye. "Maybe Cillian can take you on the weekend."

I frown. "Who's Cillian?"

"Oh, I forgot to tell you!" Betty claps her palm against her head. "My nephew, Cillian, is coming to stay with me. Well, technically he's my grand-nephew, but we don't need to acknowledge how old I'm getting."

"Is he my age, then?" I query.

"Yes. Perhaps a tad older. But he's a lovely boy. Charming. I'd better head home – he's arriving this evening, and I need to have supper ready!" She waves her loaf of bread in our direction and heads out the door.

A charming boy. I have to admit, the village is lacking young men of that description. I picture the 'lads' heading out to the lake today. It'll be Smith, who is always full of snide remarks and looking to point out any mistakes one makes. Then Helix, who travels every autumn to play flute around the country. He's very talented, but doesn't have time for anyone else. Sometimes I think he only spends time with the others to keep up the appearance of being an ordinary young man. And Haystack… I forget why we started calling him that. I guess I'd say he's sweet. But not charming. He likes knitting and once made me a scarf. It was summer. He's fat like me, but he's tall as well. I used to think I'd marry him if I never met any other contenders. But it appears I lost all interest over the years. Small village life doesn't lend itself to romance, when everyone is in everyone's business all the time.

Dad hands me a bowl of bean soup with a slice of bread. "Can you go feed your Ma? It's past twelve. She'll be getting hungry."

I take the soup into the cottage behind the bakery. Our humble abode. It's a good thing I'm an only child, because there wouldn't be room for anyone else in here. Ma and Dad have their own room, and I sleep on a bed by the fireplace in the living room.

I knock on the door to my parents' bedroom, even though I know Ma won't respond. She's sitting where she always is, facing the window, her back to the door. I wonder if she would be happier being in a different spot each day, but Dad insists she prefers the spot by the window when it's too cold to go outside.

"Ma?" I say.

Every time I call her name, I can't help but feel a flicker of hope that she'll say something in return. It's been seven years now since she became like... this. One day, she had been absolutely fine; the next, she was on the floor with no words left. The apothecarist, Heron, was hardly any help. She said that these things just happen sometimes and that there was nothing she could do.

Ma can walk with help from Dad or I, but she never chooses a direction. It's hard to tell what she's thinking, or even if she's thinking at all. Her green eyes don't reveal anything. Her long black hair is starting to show grey streaks. I inherited the black hair from her, but mine sits just below my shoulders. Hers flows down to her tailbone and always did, even before she lost her words.

"I've brought you some soup," I tell her. I kneel in front of her seat. I have to feed her, bringing each spoonful to her mouth. Occasionally it dribbles down her chin and I dab at her face with a handkerchief.

I'm ashamed that I refused to help when she first changed. Dad did everything: fed her, helped her with the chamber pot, walked her around the garden each evening, read to her, dressed and undressed her. I was too angry. I think I thought if I didn't help, it would be less real. Like it never happened.

Now, it's part of my daily routine. Dad still does the majority of the caring, but I always do lunchtimes and brush her hair at the end of the day. I offer to do more, but Dad refuses. He loves her so completely, and doing everything he can for her is his way of showing it, especially since he doesn't know if she hears his words. It's not a thankless job to him: just seeing her is reward enough.

I wonder if I'll ever love someone that much. Or be loved that wholly. I've never met anyone who made me feel that way, and if I spend my life in this village, I might not ever.

Have I ever wanted to leave the village of Schlafhold? Its cute set of cottages nestled in the forest has plenty of appeal. One main street where you can buy anything you need. A well of clean water. A few nearby hills for picnicking. And now, of course, a marvellous bridge stretching over the river and leading to the meadows beyond.

I've visited other places, including the big town of Harethorn. I say "big town", but Dad told me that a population of one thousand people is still fairly small compared to some of the distant cities. They have a main street, too, but it was so full of bustling and yelling when I visited that I almost felt I would pass out. We were there for the annual Food Market Spectacular. Dad sometimes operated a small stall there, but other times we'd gone just to experience it. We only tasted free samples, since our money was worth less there and we have never been particularly rich in the first place. But I didn't complain: I delighted in the sips of cardamom tea, the slices of fresh peaches, the nuts roasted in sugar and honey... The corners of gingerbread were my favourite. I would pinch them between my fingers and take one small bite at a time, only taking another when the ginger taste had faded from my tongue.

But I was always pleased to return home, short of breath and with aching feet from the three-day walk. Because that's what Schlafhold is. Home. Chickens in the yards and chimney smoke in the evenings. Everyone knowing your name and treating it like treasure.

There are less customers in the afternoon. Among them is Everett, who only comes in once a week or so. He's a tall, broad-shouldered man in his forties, with hairy forearms and a brown beard. He never says much. Dad knows that he's always after two brown loaves, so they never exchange a word. Everett has figured out that if you never partake in the village gossip, the gossip never latches onto you. Sure, I've heard rumours that he fought in the War for the Wilds and came back different, but that's the only morsel of information anyone has about him.

Finally, exactly one minute before closing, Poppy Pellet hurries through the door with her two children in tow.

"So sorry I'm late," she says. "Kia! Jay! Can you stand still for a moment, please?!"

The children continue to run amok, but at least they avoid knocking over any displays. All of the shelves are empty now, anyway.

"What've you got left?" Poppy asks, breathless.

Dad hesitates. Normally he keeps a couple of spare loaves under the counter, just in case we sell out. It appears that today, even those loaves have been distributed.

"I'm real sorry, Pop," says Dad. "We're about to close up, and there's nothing left."

Poppy's jaw drops. "Nothing at all?"

Dad and I shake our heads.

Poppy glances back at the children. "That's... that's okay. We got plenty of ham from the butcher's on the way here." She ushers the children out the door.

Dad turns over the sign hanging at the door so it says 'CLOSED'.

"It pains me," admits Dad, "But maybe she's learnt not to come in right as we close."

Trying to teach someone a lesson? That doesn't sound like Dad at all. He raises a hand to the back of his neck and rubs it. "I'll save some for her tomorrow."

That sounds more like him. Finding ways to be kinder.

It's a cold night in the thick of winter. I poke at the fire, willing it to warm the house faster. Dad is busy with Ma, dressing her in her nightclothes. I find myself wondering about how Smith, Helix and Haystack enjoyed their day at Haunted Lake. I've never been, but there's a painting of it in Betty's house. It's barely a quarter of a mile wide and looks quite unpleasant: dark water next to a conglomeration of rundown, abandoned buildings. The meadows along the way appear much nicer to traverse. The area to the east of Schlafhold is a lot less foresty, with open fields, rolling hills and little creeks that break off from the River Ursa.

Maybe I will go and visit the lake with this 'Cillian' who Betty has invited to the village. After all, there is not all that much to do here once you've had a stroll in the forest and a picnic on the hill.

CHAPTER 2

Poppy Pellet is first through the door the next day, beating even Prudence. Dad offers her a discount to apologise for not being able to serve her yesterday, but she refuses to take it.

Prudence comes in and speaks to me for half an hour about the traps she has put in place to stop the foxes catching her chickens. I nod along while wrapping up and bagging bread for other customers. Occasionally, I utter a "Really?" or "That sounds like a good decision", but it's hard to focus on both activities at once.

I'm offering a halfhearted "I see...", when I'm confronted by an unfamiliar smell mingling with the scent of baked bread. It's like the heavy smell of a glade deep in a forest, but without the mustiness of rotting leaves and fungi. It's... gentle and calming.

I look up to search for its source, and that's when I see him.

Slender and tall with black curls and full lips. Hazel eyes with long eyelashes. A hint of dark stubble. He's wearing a plain white shirt, but its cut is low at the front, revealing black chest hair creeping up towards his collarbone.

I've never seen him before, but it doesn't take long to realise who he is: Cillian, Betty's grand-nephew. And something about him has made my whole body feel tight.

He walks up to the counter with a relaxed gait. I notice Dad is about to turn and face him, so I quickly apologise to Prudence and shuffle along so I can be the one to serve him.

"How can I help you today?" I ask.

He smiles at me. It's such a warm, genuine smile. I notice a dimple appears in one of his cheeks.

"I heard that you occasionally have special loaves here," he says. "My aunt suggested I find out what's available today."

I panic for a moment as my mind blanks. Do we have a special today? I don't remember taking anything out of the oven besides white and brown loaves. I feel my face flushing red with embarrassment, aware that I am taking too long to answer. Why am I just standing here? Surely I can say something, anything?

Next to me, Dad steps forwards and lays his protection knife out on the bench in front of him. It's a custom when meeting and welcoming a new person. Dad's knife is as simple as they come: brown wooden handle with a silver blade. Someone gifted him something more elaborate once, but he uses it for cutting roast meat.

Cillian's protection knife, on the other hand, is more re-markable. The blade has a slight curve to it, and it's a lot shinier. The handle is blue with his name etched into the side.

"Cillian," I read out, even though I already know his name. It's the kind of name that dances in your mouth and lingers.

I hastily reach for my protection knife. It's not in the pocket of my apron, nor is it wedged in the side of my boot.

Visitors are rare to the village and it's not exactly convenient to carry a random knife when you're working all day.

I shouldn't call it a random knife. It was my mother's – still is, I suppose, but she doesn't need it. It's got a golden hilt and has the image of her as a young woman carved into it: streams of long hair, lips curved into the slightest smile, eyes looking down as she holds a snake to her bosom. I'm not sure if she ever had a snake; I think it was just fashionable at the time to be drawn with them.

After a few moments of patting my body down, I grin remorsefully. "I'm sorry I don't have my..." I spot one of the bread knives on a nearby chopping board. I quickly grab it and place it on the counter in front of me. "Will that do?"

Dad peers at me with a slight frown. He's never seen me this flustered.

The side of Cillian's mouth curls up, revealing the dimple again. "It's certainly one of the most unique protection knives I've ever seen." He eyes the long serrated edges. "Could be quite deadly, if wielded the right way."

"We've never had a reason to wield knives here," Dad says. "Not sure about where you're from."

Cillian nods and tucks his protection knife back into a sheath at his belt. "I've spent the last two and a half years at Wrensaw, helping with the rebuilding effort. We would get the occasional Twisted wandering out of the woods."

"But no human foes, I hope?" Dad asks.

Cillian shakes his head. "Back when the War for the Wilds first ended, they would get people reaching them who didn't know the War was over, or didn't want to give up even when their superiors had surrendered. But that was years ago, long before I arrived there."

I notice Cillian is missing one of his top teeth: fourth one along on the right.

I want to know what it was like in Wrensaw. What he did there. I want to know how long he's staying here, and if he'll meet with me later. I want to know what it feels like to stand just a little bit closer to him...

My own thoughts set me off balance. What am I doing? I finally, *finally* remember where it all began.

"Today's special is a seedy loaf," I declare, offering up a paper bag containing a seed-studded loaf.

"Looks delicious." Cillian trades it for a handful of coins. He heads towards the door, but then stops to look back. "I didn't catch your name!"

"Minnow," I reply.

"It was a pleasure meeting you, Minnow."

As *if* Betty didn't already tell him my name.

"Minnow." It's Dad saying my name this time.

"Yes?"

"Where's your protection knife?"

"Come on, you know we don't need-..."

"That's not why I'm asking."

"Oh." Of course. It's Ma's knife, not mine. "I'm sorry. I think it's by my bed."

Dad nods in the direction of the house. He doesn't need to say a word. I get the message.

As I expected, my protection knife is lying under the edge of my bed. Just as I'm slipping it into a sheath, I hear:

"Minnow?"

It's my Ma's voice.

I rush to her room as fast as I can.

But when I get there, she looks the same as always. Seated on the chair, staring out the window blankly, totally silent except for her soft breathing.

I kneel in front of her and take her hand in mine. I rub it softly.

"Ma? Did you say something?"

No response.

"I'm here, Ma. If you want me, I'm here. What do you need?"

I wait a few minutes, but there is no sign that she ever made a sound to begin with.

I head back to the bakery.

"You found your knife?" asks Dad.

I nod. I open my mouth to tell him about Ma talking, but change my mind. I don't want to give him false hope. If I say something, he'll think of nothing else for weeks. He won't leave her side, in case she speaks again. The stress isn't good for him.

So, I continue my day as per usual. Well, not entirely as per usual. I still have Cillian Gray on my mind.

CHAPTER 3

I don't see Cillian for a few days. I begin to worry that he's gone back to Wrensaw, or wherever it is his travels are taking him next. Betty comes in to buy bread, but I resist the urge to ask about him. I don't want to seem too interested.

It's not until three days after our initial meeting, as I'm practically skipping down the street towards the well (clumsily but with whimsy in my heart), that I spot him strolling down the street towards me.

I quickly adjust my speed and gait so I'm walking normally.

He's already standing up straight – it seems to be his natural posture – but he somehow manages to become even straighter and taller when he sees me.

"Good morning, Minnow!" he calls. There's that dimple again.

"Good morning, Cillian," I echo.

"I'm hoping you can help me with something – oh, wait, it appears you're busy." He nods to the empty bucket I'm holding.

"No, it's okay!" I assure him. I try not to cringe at the way my voice lilts into a higher octave than usual. "What do you need?"

He pulls a small piece of paper from his pocket and unfolds it. "I've been examining a map of the area, but it appears to be missing a few locations."

I step closer and stand beside him. I can feel his arm hairs against mine, and it sends a shiver through me. If I lean the slightest bit to the left, our skin will touch.

"So, here's Schlafhold," he indicates, pointing at our current location. "To the north is forest, until you get to Byrne. I'm assuming that's the village I passed through on my way down?"

"Yes. They're known for their tomatoes."

"Then to the west," continues Cillian, "More forest, unsurprisingly."

"There's a path going through," I explain, "And a few houses along the way. Old people sometimes move there if they're tired of village life. Eventually the forest ends and the path reaches the Amber City. But I've never been that far."

"I see. And to the south? My map doesn't show much."

I hesitate. "No-one goes south. There's nothing there."

"Surely there must be *something* there."

"Trees," I answer.

Cillian looks at me, his right eye squinting in curiosity.

I continue, "Some people say that if you travel far south enough, you reach the end of the world."

Cillian tosses his head back and laughs.

I feel my face flushing with embarrassment. I mutter quietly, "I didn't say *I* believe it."

Cillian stops laughing and lets out a sigh. "No... I mean, the world has to end somewhere, right?" He gazes in the direction of south.

"But they don't just mean the land," I say. "They mean time, as well. Existence."

Cillian appears more serious now. Confused. "What do you mean?"

"Well, that's where the Twisteds live," I reply. "The further south you go, the more of them there are."

Cillian cocks his head to the side. "So... there's a point where it's impossible to go further because there are too many of them?"

"If they outweigh the number of people, isn't that the end for us? If we all went down there, it would be over. No more humans. So it's the end."

Cillian's hand absentmindedly goes to the knife at his belt. "Have you ever seen a Twisted?"

I shake my head. "I only know about them from storybooks." The stories are enough to assure me that I never want to encounter one. Gangly creatures with limbs like gnarly, knotted tree branches. Long, vertical eyes with huge pupils for seeing in the dark forests. They have dog-like teeth and aim for the legs so you can't run.

"I hope you never have to see one," says Cillian. "It's terrifying, even if you think you know what to expect."

"You said you had to fight them at Wrensaw?"

"It was hardly me. I caused a few wounds, but it was the other warriors who did the bulk of the work. My job in Wrensaw was mainly moving materials around to help with re-building the houses."

For some reason, this makes me like him more. He clearly has a charitable streak. And now that I'm standing closer to him, I can see the muscles in his arms that he must have culti-vated while lugging building materials around all day. I won-der if I could beat him in an arm wrestle. I think I'd give him a run for his money – lifting big sacks of flour each day has built up my strength over the years.

"My main interest today, though," says Cillian, "Is what lies to the east."

His map ends abruptly at the eastern edge of Schlafhold, before even reaching the bridge. He taps the edge of the paper.

"I'm sure you can get a better map from Mr Gust," I sug-gest, pointing in the direction of Mr Gust's miscellaneous goods shop.

Cillian sighs and appears to crumple a bit. "Yes, I'm sure you're right. Thanks anyway, Minnow." He puts the map back in his pocket and begins to walk away. Oh, now I've re-ally made a mistake.

"Wait!" I call after him, louder than I need to. "I can tell you about the east, if you like. I'd be useless at drawing, that's all."

Cillian grins. "That's okay. I just need a rough idea."

"So there's the bridge," I explain. "Then, there are a few miles of meadows. Not many people live out there at the mo-ment. Just a few farms. Then there's Walnut Woods to the northeast. They're quite different to this forest. The village of

Yammoor is somewhere in there, too. But if you keep travelling straight east, you reach Haunted Lake."

"I've heard of Haunted Lake."

"It's just a lake surrounded by some ruins. I think people make it out to sound more exciting than it actually is."

"Have you been?"

"No," I admit.

"So, how do you know it's not exciting?"

"My Dad said so."

"It sounds like you value his opinion a lot."

I shrug. "He's my Dad. He's always taken good care of me. Haven't your parents?"

A flicker of pain crosses Cillian's face, and I realise it's a question I shouldn't have asked.

He quickly changes the subject. "So if Haunted Lake is surrounded by ruins, what used to be there?"

I frown, racking my brain for an answer. Did I study the history of the area in school? For some reason, not a single response emerges from my mind. "I have no idea."

Cillian nods slowly. "Aunt Betty didn't seem to know much either." He grins. "A mystery to be solved, I suppose. Are you fond of mysteries, Minnow?"

Am I? Most of my day is occupied with nothing but thoughts of work, and my evenings are normally spent with my family. Saturdays, my day off, consist of meeting with my friend Thivya and keeping ourselves busy by berry-picking, picnicking, sewing, and catching up with the local gossip while drinking tea with Betty and some of the frailer women in town. They love doing our hair and telling stories from their youth (even though we've heard them several times already). Sometimes we help the neighbours with chores such as repairing chicken coops and repainting walls. There's always something to do and someone who can use a little help if you're in the mood to give it.

But solving mysteries? That would be something entirely new.

"I don't mind a good mystery," I say, downplaying my interest. I don't want to seem inexperienced.

"Wonderful," says Cillian. "Maybe it's a mystery we can solve together. Are you free on Sunday?"

"Bakery's open on Sundays," I answer. "I have Saturdays off."

"You work six days a week?"

I nod.

"That's a lot of pressure. You must get tired."

Now that I think about it, he's right. Saturdays give me just enough time to replenish my strength, and then it's the same thing all over again. I've gotten used to enduring the work days, but why shouldn't I have more time for leisure? None of the other people my age work as much.

I shrug. "It's how it's always been."

"I can't do Saturday because I need to take Betty out of town for the day," explains Cillian. "But if you can make yourself free on Sunday... I'd love to spend the day with you."

It won't be that hard, right? I can miss a day at the bakery. Sundays are usually a busier day, since people are stocking up for the week ahead. But Dad can handle it. Anyway, I'm an adult. I can expect a day off every now and then.

"Sure," I say.

It's decided.

I tell Dad my plan in the evening, after he has put Ma to bed.

"But the bakery is open on Sundays," is Dad's first response.

"I *know* that. But I think it's fair for me to get a day off. And I want to get to know Cillian."

Dad narrows his eyes. "I think you've learnt enough. He's Betty's grand-nephew. He's worked in Wrensaw. And he'll probably leave town again soon."

"It's more than that. He's the first interesting man my age I have ever met. I could at least use another friend, if nothing else."

"And... he's just a friend?"

"I've met him twice. Yes, he's just a friend."

Dad chews on his bottom lip. "Alright."

Relief floods through me.

"But," Dad continues. "I don't like the idea of you going to Haunted Lake."

I roll my eyes. "Are you serious? Smith and his friends went out there the other day. And you said you used to go there."

"Yes, but we're..." He hesitates, and then cringes. "We're men."

As soon as he says it, he knows he's lost the argument.

I lift my head up high. "Oh, is that it?"

"Fine," grumbles Dad. "But I need you back at the bakery first thing Monday morning!"

"Understood."

"Wait, I didn't mean that. Be back Sunday night!"

"Don't worry, Dad. I know you'd miss me too much if I wasn't back that night."

CHAPTER 4

I meet up with Thivya on Saturday as per usual. She's brought a ball and pins, so we set up a game of bowling near the new bridge. The grass is nice and flat here, and the smell of morning dew permeates the air. It almost cancels out the odour from the nearby stables. The sun is peeking out from behind light grey clouds, promising a mild winter day that will be warm by the afternoon.

Thivya is especially focused on the game today. We've played three times over the past two months, and she is determined to keep up her winning streak. She's not usually the competitive type. But now she's tasted success, she doesn't want to let it go.

Thivya is the more outgoing out of the two of us, and I would argue she is sweeter as well, in her own way. She's the oldest of five children and spends most of her time caring for her siblings while her parents work. Her brown skin appears to be glowing in the light today as she grins at my first miss of the game.

"Come on, Minnow, you can do better than that," she chides. "No need to go easy on me."

Her luck isn't any better, but it doesn't matter. Laughing together and feeling the warmth of companionship is what makes our Saturdays perfect.

Just as I earn my first point of the game, the sound of a voice crying out draws our attention.

"Where did that come from?" asks Thivya, frowning.

I look around, but there's no-one in sight. The village looks still.

"Over the bridge, I guess," I say. "Do you want to check it out?"

Thivya hesitates.

The voice cries out again. The words are clearer this time: "Help! Help us!"

It's coming from the other side of the bridge.

Thivya and I exchange alarmed glances and then put down our game equipment. We hurry over to the bridge and see three figures at the other side, slowly making their way towards us.

It doesn't take me long to recognise them: Smith, Helix and Haystack. Haystack and Smith are supporting Helix, who has an arm around each of their shoulders as he limps forwards.

My first thought is that Helix must have tripped and hurt his ankle. Hopefully he hasn't broken his leg. That would take ages to heal.

But then I see the blood. All the blood soaking his left leg's trousers, which have been ripped up. I've never seen anything like it. The sight makes me feel sick, but at the same time, I can't look away.

"We should help," Thivya says, with a shakiness in her voice.

"What can we even do?" I ask, at a loss. I'm too shocked to think of how to respond.

"I'll get someone – Everett – to come help carry Helix," says Thivya. "You go and tell Heron that Helix will need help."

I nod and head into the village. Heron, the apothecarist, has a house on the far side of town. She's a talented healer, at least when it comes to common colds and scratches needing stitches. I wonder if she's ever treated anything like whatever Helix is suffering. The image of the gash along his thigh with bits of skin peeling off appears unbidden in my mind. I hope it doesn't give me nightmares.

I reach Heron's house and knock on the door urgently. When she doesn't answer, I bang it harder.

Finally, she emerges, wearing a green headscarf and rubbing at her eye. She's a short woman with olive skin and a round face. "You woke me."

I glance up at the sky. I'd say it is only two hours before midday. But that's irrelevant right now.

"Helix is on the way," I inform her. "Something's happened to him."

"Well? What?"

"I don't know," I admit. "But he's bleeding... a lot. From his leg. It looked like something had torn into him... A bear, maybe?"

"There are no bears near here," Heron says, with a shake of her head.

"They came from the other side of the bridge," I explain. "So maybe they went into... the woods north of there... I don't know."

I am suddenly aware of how puffed I am. I'm straining to get my words out. I notice how wheezy my next breath sounds. Heron does too.

"Oh , Minnow," she says. "Here, come and sit on the stool."

I take the stool and place it in front of the table in the corner. I do what she taught me to do when I was a child: lean forwards, breathe in and out of my nose, keeping my chest and shoulders as still as possible.

"Just the stomach ," Heron reminds me. "No breathing into the chest. Slower. Slower."

I can hear her boiling water in the background.

"Now, breathe out," she continues. "Hold your breath until I say to release. Do not breathe in again."

I hold at her command.

"Now, breathe back in," Heron instructs after ten seconds.

We repeat this a few times until my breathing begins to feel normal again.

"It's been a while since you had an episode, isn't it?" asks Heron.

"It's been a while since I ran that fast," I chuckle, and then cough from the laughing.

Heron brings over a bowl of boiled water and gets me to inhale the steam. Based on how long I've been here, I figure that Helix and the others must be about to arrive. Heron has already busied herself preparing bandages, cleaning sharp implements, and grinding pastes with a pestle and mortar.

I know I shouldn't ask, but I venture the question that I can't help bringing up with Heron. "I don't suppose you've heard anything about new treatments that... you know. Anything that could help Ma."

Heron turns to me with a sad smile. "As always, Minnow, if anything reaches me, I will come knocking on your door straightaway."

"Thank you," I say.

"You take care, now."

I cross the street and look on as Everett and Haystack escort Helix into Heron's house. Smith lingers behind, looking yellow. I go over to him.

"You alright?"

Smith raises his head as if to nod, but then quickly shakes his head.

"What happened?" I ask. "I told Heron it might have been a bear. It looked awful."

"Not a bear," says Smith, his voice quiet and breathy.

More villagers emerge onto the street, having heard the noise as people passed through. Among them is Betty, carrying a large bag. She was clearly ready to leave for the day. Beside her is Cillian, wearing a travelling cap.

Cillian strides up to us. I notice how serene he looks with his lilac shirt's sleeves rolled up to his elbows.

"Is Helix okay?" asks Cillian.

"I don't... I don't know," replies Smith. "But we're never going back to Haunted Lake."

Cillian peers closely at him. "Why not? What was there?"

Smith hesitates, then, "A Twisted." He says it louder, so more villagers can hear. "There was a Twisted at Haunted Lake."

A shocked murmur emanates from the onlookers.

I look at Cillian. He meets my gaze, but I can't tell what he's thinking. I guess we're not going tomorrow after all.

Smith sits down in the dirt suddenly, shaking his head.

Cillian crouches beside him. "How do you know it was a Twisted?"

"Don't you believe me?"

"That's not what I'm saying. What did it look like?"

Smith stares at Cillian blankly. "It... it grabbed Helix's leg and we had to pull him free. What else could have done that to him? We were walking through the ruins and something – the Twisted – came out from behind a wall. Ask Haystack. He'll say the same thing."

Cillian nods and stands back up. I can tell he's not convinced.

Smith isn't paying him any attention, though. He has drawn his knees up to his chest and tears are starting to trickle down his face. It makes me deeply uncomfortable seeing the man who is usually so tough and snarky appear so fragile and shaken.

Thivya arrives and assesses the scene. She knows that Smith hasn't exactly treated me well over the years. And, as much as I wouldn't wish his situation on anyone, I'm definitely not the right person to be comforting him right now.

Thivya nods at me. "I've got this." Looking after people is her superpower.

I start walking away. Cillian catches up to me.

"Tomorrow, then," he says.

"I know. It's a real shame." I sigh.

"You don't want to go?"

"What?! You do?"

Cillian shrugs. "I need to go. Twisted or not. Don't you trust me to protect you?" He taps the knife at his belt.

"Maybe I can protect myself," I grumble, although it's several months since I did any kind of training. "Anyway, what do you mean you *need* to go?"

Cillian looks over to where Betty is and sees she is engaged in animated chatter with the other villagers.

"Come with me," he says, and starts heading towards the edge of the forest.

Once under the cover of trees, Cillian turns to me.

"What I'm about to tell you can't be shared with anyone," he says, tilting his head down so his eyes are looking directly into mine. Such colourful eyes. Green and brown and gold. Leaf and syrup and sun. "Can you promise me you'll keep it to yourself?" he asks.

"You haven't even told me what it is, yet," I say with a smile.

His gaze is humourless. "Minnow. I'm serious. No-one can know a thing. Not even your Dad."

It's not often I'm told to keep secrets. There are hardly any secrets in a village like Schlafhold.

"I promise."

Cillian takes a deep breath in. "I'm Cursed."

I stare at him, waiting for more of an explanation. What does he mean?

He continues, "A Witch placed a Curse on me."

"What's the Curse?" I ask. Whoops, maybe that was too personal a question. Come on, Minnow. Show some sensitivity.

Cillian sighs. "Unless I complete a Counterspell, I can never see my son again. Any time I get close, fate intervenes and he ends up elsewhere."

"You have a son?!" I exclaim. Ugh, Minnow, sensitivity, remember? "I mean – I'm really sorry to hear about that. It must be difficult being unable to see him."

"Torturous," agrees Cillian. "He's only one year old. There was a woman I met in Wrensaw. She was a military captain, only passing through for a few days to check on the rebuilding progress." Cillian's eyes glaze over as he recollects the past. "We drank too much ale. Got too close. We had plenty in common. Both wanted to travel, both liked long discussions about the meaning of life, both came from well-known families."

I feel a momentary ache of jealousy. Will Cillian have any interest in me at all if I am none of those things? Can you be friends with someone so different to you? But Cillian must like me, at least a little bit. Otherwise, he wouldn't be sharing his secret with me.

Cillian continues. "It was a mistake. We knew that before she had even left. I went to see her when she had the baby."

His throat tightens, and he takes a moment to compose himself. "His heart kept stopping. He was so tiny. And his heart kept stopping. She was devoted to her job and didn't want to stay and be a mother. I think she truly loved him, but the boy's condition made her feel she hadn't done it right. She had such high standards for herself."

"Where is she now?"

"A high-ranking general. Still travelling. I've only seen her once since the weeks after our son's birth. She spoke to me as if there had never been anything between us."

"And your son?"

"It broke my heart seeing him suffer. I couldn't let him die. So I did what I had to, even though his mother did not approve of it. I went to a Witch."

"And she said you could never see him again."

"Yes. For every Spell, every Blessing, there is a price to pay. He was mended. I was Cursed. I could never lay eyes on him again. He lives with my mother and sister now. But I've learnt of a Counterspell."

"To do with Haunted Lake?"

"I have to collect a number of items that can combine to create the Counterspell. I need three black stones from the bottom of Haunted Lake."

I wince. "You have to actually go in the water?"

"Afraid so." He pauses. "That's why I have to go to Haunted Lake. And why I was hoping you could help me. But I understand if you don't want to see me again, now that you know about my Curse."

"No, of course I do!" I reply. "The Curse doesn't matter to me. You're still... you."

He smiles appreciatively, and there's a warmth in his gaze that makes me feel like I'm soaking in a hot bath.

"If I can't go to Haunted Lake with you, I'll still help with the other things," I say.

"Really? I could use all the help I can get."

"What else do you need?"

"There are three other things: the flesh of a Blessed orange, a hair from a black goat, and a vial of water from a spring by a willow tree."

"You need something already Blessed?"

"To counterbalance the Curse ingredient, I suppose. Not sure where I'll find a Blessed orange, though."

"I might know," I say, recalling eating fine fruits at Harethorn's Food Market Spectacular. "As for a spring by a willow tree... Surely there's one in the forest?"

We glance around, even though we both already know there isn't a willow tree in sight. The forest is thick with oaks.

"Maybe not here," I say. "But Walnut Woods across the bridge and to the north might have one. There's a lot more diversity there – animals, different plants, fungi."

Cillian nods thoughtfully. "Perhaps that's where we go tomorrow?"

"Sounds like a plan."

CHAPTER 5

"It's not safe to go anywhere at the moment," Dad dictates as he cleans the dishes after dinner. "If there was a Twisted at Haunted Lake, who knows what else is out there?" He shakes his head in disbelief. "I trust you'll be staying put tomorrow?"

"I'm still going to see Cillian."

Dad narrows his eyes. "And what'll you be doing with him?"

"I don't know. Maybe go for a walk."

"Walk where?"

"Ugh! Dad, can you give me some space?" I shoot him a venomous glare.

He looks taken aback and slightly hurt. I instantly regret my outburst.

Dad looks down at the glass he is drying with a tea towel. "Just tryna keep you safe, Min," he says, softly. "Just promise me you're not heading out to Haunted Lake."

"I promise."

"I have my reservations about this Cillian chap, too."

"What? Why?"

"He's just... a stranger, isn't he? He's shown a lot of interest in you very quickly."

"I've gotten to know him, so he's not exactly a stranger. Do you think people shouldn't show interest in me?"

Dad sighs. "You know that's not what I mean, Minnow." He places the glass on the kitchen bench. "You have a good day tomorrow, hey? You deserve a good day. I'll be here for you when you get back."

Cillian meets me by the bridge. The weather isn't as fine as yesterday, but I think the rain will hold off. It's still early. My breath is foggy when I exhale.

He's wearing a fur-lined black overcoat along with tan animal-skin trousers.

My wardrobe isn't nearly as variable as his, particularly since I usually wear a baker's outfit and apron six days a week. However, today I've got a sky blue blouse that used to belong to Ma. I've tried to adjust it to fit my size, but the job is a bit patchy. I'm wearing it with a shin-length grey skirt and black boots. Simple, but nicer than a uniform. A belt at my waist holds my protection knife.

Cillian and I start walking together after a brief greeting.

We make our way to the bridge, waving at Prudence on the way as she pulls up carrots in her garden.

After crossing the bridge, we follow the faint path north that leads to Walnut Woods. We pass a pasture hosting a couple of brown cows. To my dismay, it starts raining for a moment; but it quickly subsides. I shiver a little.

"Would you like my jacket?" asks Cillian.

"I'm fine-..." I begin, but Cillian has already draped it around my shoulders. It's like a **warm** hug I could live in forever. It carries that deep-forest smell of his, too. I try not to make it too obvious that I'm inhaling a deep breath of it. It's such a simple smell, but intoxicating at the same time. It makes it hard to think straight.

I begin a conversation to re-establish my focus. "How did you find a Witch, anyway?" I ask. "One passed through our village once, but I wouldn't know where to seek one out."

"They're where you would expect them to be," answers Cillian. "Rotting log cabins deep in the woods. Lone cottages atop cliffs by the sea. Lamplit hovels in the middle of swamps. Huts hidden high among snow-capped mountains. But in a way, they find you. I sought one out in a forest, and she met me in a dark glade before I had even reached the place I'd heard of."

"What was she like?"

"Ageless," responds Cillian. "Each time I looked at her face, I couldn't tell if she was young or old. The veins visible through the skin on her hands were deep blue. She was dressed in all black, with wide billowy clothes that blew in the wind like kites." He frowns. "Now that I think about it, it was a calm day. She brought the wind with her."

"She wasn't wearing a veil?"

"No. When she placed the Blessing – and the Curse – she went into a kind of trance and her eyes turned yellow with the pupil slitted like a black cat. It scared me so much I almost ran away. But she wasn't... cruel. She was just doing what I had asked, really. She listened closely and made sure I understood what would happen. It didn't feel like trickery."

"You don't think she was evil, then?"

"What makes something evil? Practising dark arts? Or the way you use them? I try not to think too hard about it. My Curse feels evil. I worry it means there is evil attached to me."

We've reached Walnut Woods. The tree boughs here are smoother and greyer than the other forest. There is more space between the trees. A sweet whistling bird call pierces the air.

A sizeable buzzing bee surges past, a little too close for my liking. I leap away from it and bump into Cillian. I quickly step away again, but not before I feel my cheeks turning red. To my surprise, Cillian also launches himself away from the bee, inhaling sharply.

"Sorry about that," I apologise. "I've been stung a few times in the past."

"No, I don't blame you. The things terrify me."

"They do?"

"Yes. Give me a Twisted any day." He chuckles. "Anything else dangerous I should be worried about?"

I rack my brains. It's been a while since I've visited these woods.

"There's bears," I say. "But they haven't attacked anyone from the village for at least fifty years. You just walk away if you see one. Haystack saw an adder once, but it just slithered under a log."

Mud clings to the base of my shoes as we trudge further into the woods. Cillian appears to be enjoying the sights and sounds. He looks up at every bird call and touches the bark of any trees we wander close to. One time, he spends a moment crouching down to marvel at a purple lichen-like growth covering a tree trunk.

"You can't be in that much of a hurry to break this Curse," I joke.

Cillian stands up. "I can't let it control my every waking moment. That's like letting it win. I have to embrace the rest of life as well." He pauses. "I think we should head down into that valley. It looks like the sort of place a spring would form."

This area is more open with less trees. There's no path down, so we have to beat bushes aside. Sometimes I struggle to keep my balance, and I try not to grab onto Cillian for support. Honestly, that would probably just result in both of us tumbling to the ground and rolling around like overturned turtles in a bed of brambles.

Then, up ahead, I see a trio of trees with long, hair-like strings hanging down and almost touching the ground in places. The branches are bereft of leaves, but the type of tree is unmistakable.

"Willow," I say under my breath.

We make towards the trees with haste, hoping to find a spring beyond.

However, just before we reach them, a whistling sound makes me freeze. Something soars past my eyes, and I instinctively stagger backwards and cover my face, recalling the bee from earlier.

Hearing no further noise, I slowly lower my hand.

I look over to Cillian and see that he is slowly drawing his protection knife.

"What...?" I murmur.

He silently nods to the closest willow tree. An arrow is embedded in the trunk.

The realisation that I almost lost my nose a few moments ago makes my chest tingle uncomfortably. I draw my protection knife as well, although I know it won't be of any use against an archer who wants us dead.

"Who else goes into this forest?" whispers Cillian.

"I don't know... We could be near the village of Yammoor."

"We need to move," says Cillian decidedly, backing away in the direction we came from.

"But what about the willow trees? There could be water right on the other side."

Cillian's gaze flickers between the willow trees and the direction the arrow came from.

"Come on," I say. "We can be quick."

Cillian is still hesitating. The sound of movement through the bushes in the distance begins to reach us.

"Here, give me the vial," I say, holding out a hand and putting my protection knife away. "I'm shorter than you, so I'll be harder to spot."

Cillian is decent enough not to remark that while, yes, I am shorter, I am also a lot wider. He presses a glass vial into my hand. It is smaller and lighter than I expected.

I trample a few more bushes before reaching the willow trees.

"Someone's coming," I hear Cillian call to me. I hear the sound of another arrow swooshing through the air.

The ground gets muddier and squelchy beneath my boots. I smile. Mud means water. A smallish spring of water sits in front of me, quiet and serene. A few birds are perched on the banks at the opposite side.

I kneel down at the edge of the water and fill the vial as quickly as I can. Once it's full, I place the cork stopper in.

I make my way back to Cillian with a victorious grin on my face.

He's not there.

I glance around, but he's nowhere in sight.

Should I wait for him to come back? Surely he hasn't abandoned me?

My breath quickens as I struggle to grasp my options. Stay here until Cillian comes back for me – or until I get found by someone who wants to harm me. Head back towards Schlafhold alone, hoping that Cillian isn't lying half-dead nearby and depending on me to rescue him. Or go in search of our attackers and give them a piece of my mind with my trusty protection knife.

I decide to avoid the latter and instead slowly pick my way through the woods, keeping an eye and ear out for Cillian. I note another arrow wedged into the bark of a tree and spot shoe prints in the mud. Cillian's? Or an archer looking to see what they'd hit?

There's no sign of blood, at least. I follow the direction of the footprints, keeping them in view as I weave my way through trees and shrubs. The track becomes a steep incline, and I begin to feel pressure on my lungs. I don't want to stop, but I know I have to regulate my breathing or I'll never be able to breathe again when I reach the top of the hill. Heron is not here to help me.

A minute passes. Finally, I feel recovered enough to continue.

At last, the ground levels out. That's when I see them, straight ahead:

Cillian pinned to the ground by a stocky, moustached man wearing brown leather gloves. Cillian's nearest hand is red and swollen.

The man appears to slap Cillian in the face, and Cillian writhes underneath his weight. Then, the man pulls out a knife and begins to aim it at Cillian's face. The blade lowers...

"No! Stop!" I cry out, drawing my knife. It feels light in my hand as my body reacts to the excitement of the moment.

As I begin to charge towards them, a woman with waist-long brown hair steps out from behind a tree, blocking my path. She has a bow and immediately points an arrow in my direction.

CHAPTER 6

I freeze where I am. I suppose I could throw my knife at the woman, but the chances are I'd miss and then I'd be dead for sure.

"It's okay, Minnow," calls Cillian. Then, to the man, "She's with me."

The woman doesn't budge.

Cillian pipes up again, "Minnow, put away your knife."

Reluctantly, I tuck my knife back into its sheath. I feel exposed standing unarmed in front of the woman. She doesn't budge.

Finally, the man says in a twangy voice, "Leave her, Abby."

The woman's gaze doesn't move from me, but she lowers the bow and places the arrow back in her quiver. I notice that despite her glare and clenched jaw, she is actually quite pretty with her long, oval-shaped face and deep brown eyes. She is average height and build, with broad shoulders and arm muscles that are obviously toned from practising archery.

After a moment, she silently steps aside.

I hurry over to where Cillian is lying. A red blotch marks his cheek.

The moustached man, still straddling him, leans backwards and looks up at me. "There's just one stinger left. Then you can have him back."

I watch as the man uses his knife-tip to flick a tiny black bee stinger from Cillian's cheek.

Cillian lets out a relieved exhale. The man gets off him.

Cillian remains on the ground, breathing deeply.

It all falls into place. The man wasn't attacking Cillian – he was helping remove bee stingers. He didn't slap him – he was swatting a bee away. And Cillian, terrified of bees as he is, had been panicking and needed to be held down.

The man holds out his protection knife in my direction, hilt facing me. "I'm Derek, from Yammoor. This here is Abby, my daughter. Sorry for scaring you earlier. There aren't normally people in the woods. We saw your figures in the valley and assumed you were deer." He chuckles harshly. "Hopefully looking after your friend here makes up for our indiscretion."

"You... almost killed us," I say, remembering the first arrow that soared past me.

Derek winces. "Yes. Sorry about that." He takes a waterskin from his pocket and starts splashing water onto Cillian's stings. "That feel better?"

Cillian nods.

I unsheathe my protection knife and hold the hilt facing Derek, as custom demands when showing friendship. It's a sign that you won't harm them and you are trusting them not to harm you. I point the hilt in Abby's direction as well.

With a steely look in her eye, she draws hers and does the same. Her blade is sparkling silver and the hilt is decorated with leaf patterns.

Cillian gets to his feet. He briefly inspects the welts on his arm.

I put my knife away again. "We'd better get going," I say.

Cillian sighs. "I guess we failed our quest."

"What do you mean?" I ask.

"We didn't get what we came for."

"You mean this?" I hold up the vial of water.

Cillian's face lights up. "Well done, Minnow."

Abby and Derek exchange confused looks.

Cillian turns to them. "We'll head back to Schlafhold now. I hope you find a deer! And thank you heartily for your help with the stings."

Derek beams. "Anytime, friend."

Cillian nods respectfully in Abby's direction. I'm not sure what to do, so I copy him and then follow as he departs.

"That was a strange encounter," I mutter as soon as we are out of earshot.

"Yes, both lucky and unlucky," observes Cillian.

I hand him the vial of spring water. He quickly pockets it.

"Thanks," he says with a warm smile, complete with dimple and missing tooth.

There's something about his smile that makes me feel so… seen. That's what Cillian does. He makes me feel seen.

Dad is waiting inside for me when I get home. It's on the darker side of sunset. My skirt is studded with burrs and brambles. My boots are caked in mud. There's dirt underneath my fingernails – I'll have to get all of that out before I'm allowed near any dough.

"You said you wouldn't go to Haunted Lake," says Dad, crossing his arms.

"I didn't go," I respond, closing the door.

"Prudence saw you crossing the bridge with Cillian."

"Oh, you're spying on me now, are you?"

"You promised."

"And I kept my promise! I didn't go anywhere near Haunted Lake," I insist. I can tell by the look in Dad's eyes that he doesn't believe me. I continue, "Maybe you should get Prudence to follow us all the way next time. She can tag along while we spend the day together. I'm sure we'd all have so much fun."

Dad doesn't respond. He just stands there, staring at me.

"Why won't you believe me? If you have to know, we went to Walnut Woods."

"Alone?"

"What does it matter? Yes, alone. Besides some people from Yammoor we met."

Dad hesitates. Then, he looks down to the floor. "I'm sorry."

"For?"

"I shouldn't have doubted you. It was unfair. You've never lied to me."

He's right. I mean, I've hidden things. Like Ma talking the other day. But I've never stated a lie to his face.

For some reason, I feel my throat tighten with emotion. "I'm gonna go brush Ma's hair," I manage, holding back unbidden tears.

Ma is sitting as still as ever by the fire. The flickering light reflects off her irises. I take my time brushing her hair, being careful with every black strand. I remember the days when she would do the same for me. I would wriggle and writhe, hating the feeling as a young child.

What I would give to have that back again.

Dad enters, carrying a plate of potatoes and green beans for me.

"I can feed Ma as well," I offer, "Since I wasn't here at lunch."

Dad shakes his head. "I'll do it. It's my job."

I don't argue. I know by now how precious each moment with her is to him.

CHAPTER 7

It's Monday morning, and I'm tying the strings of my apron when there is a sharp rap at the door to the bakery. I squint out the window in confusion, as it's not opening time yet.

Standing in front of the door is Heron, shivering slightly in the morning chill.

I open the door. "Heron? Please, come in out of the cold."

Heron smiles gratefully and steps inside, loosening her grip on her headscarf. "Oh, it smells lovely in here."

"Ha, tell me about it."

"Minnow, I told you I would come knocking on your door if I ever heard about anything that could help your Ma."

My heart rate quickens. I lean in closer to her, worrying that my ears could inexplicably lose their strength at any moment.

Heron takes a deep breath. "I don't want to get your hopes up too much. But word has reached me of a travelling healer who has incredible capabilities. They say he has brought people back from the brink of death. If anyone could help your Ma, it's him."

"And he's travelling here?"

Heron sighs and shakes her head. "No. He's from far up north. I heard he's passing through Harethorn in a week. But that's the closest he'll get to Schlafhold."

I try to think through a plan – timing, travel, people, places... but my brain whirrs so fast that it gets stuck. The gears won't turn.

"Are you okay, love?" asks Heron.

I become aware of the fact I am standing on the spot looking like a stunned bird. "I..." I begin, but it's all I can get out.

"Like I said, I don't want to give you false hope. But I would be doing wrong to not tell you.'

She reaches for my hand and gives it a little pat.

Will I be able to get my Ma back? Would she be the same after all these years?

One thing at a time.

"Thank you," I say to Heron.

I linger by the door after Heron leaves. Don't get my hopes up? I haven't felt this hopeful in a long time.

Dad, unaware of Heron's visit, enters and starts kneading dough at the counter.

"Minnow? What's wrong?"

I turn to him. "There's a travelling healer passing through Harethorn next week."

He doesn't look up. "They have their big markets on, don't they? The Spectacular? I told them we couldn't go this year. Too much work here."

"Heron said this healer was special. She said he might be able to help Ma."

Dad goes as still as a statue, knuckles pressed down into soft dough.

"I thought at first we could take Ma to see him," I explain, "But I think that would be too difficult. So, maybe it would be better if I travel up on my own and convince him to come down here."

Dad doesn't respond.

"I know he'll probably want money," I continue. "I could have a stall at the markets. Like we used to do." I step closer to him.

Dad looks down. "You know what I said. No more doctors, no more healers, no more apothecarists. No more nonsense."

"Heron said-..."

"Heron hasn't helped us," interrupts Dad. "She didn't seven years ago, and she doesn't now."

"Please, Dad. You don't have to go. You don't have to think about it. But let me try. If I don't at least try, I'll be left wondering forever if I missed the chance to help her."

Dad grits his teeth. I know he's trying not to show emotion. Finally, "You can't travel alone."

"Cillian would come, if I asked him."

Dad looks up at me. "Is there no-one else who could go?"

"Like who?"

"I don't know. Thivya?"

"You know she has to look after her siblings. Anyway, what's wrong with me going with Cillian? He has business in Harethorn to attend to as well. It's good timing."

Dad says nothing for a while, and then shakes his head. "We need you here. I need you. Your Ma needs you. You'd be gone for over a week. How am I meant to run the bakery by myself and look after her on my own for that long?"

"Yes, how would you do it?" I question. "Is this what you expect of me? To just spend the rest of my life in this bakery?" This isn't where I intended the argument to go, but now the idea has occurred to me, I let it ripen. "Maybe I want to do more with my life. Maybe I don't want to be trapped here forever, in the same daily routine, seeing all the same people and doing all the same chores. Maybe there's more for me out there!"

Dad looks at me with a bewildered expression. "Where's this coming from? It's because of that boy, isn't it?"

"It has nothing to do with him," I retort.

Dad clenches his fists and starts kneading the dough again with vigour. "You really want to leave us?"

A feeling of guilt begins to curl in my stomach, but I don't back down. "I think I have a right to."

Dad grabs the ball of dough and squeezes it hard. I know it's frustration and not anger. Or maybe it is anger. But he doesn't raise his voice at me. Instead, he shrugs. "Go, then."

It's a simple phrase, but it means so much more. *Go, then. Abandon us. Neglect your family.*

"I'll come back," I say. "With the healer, if I can. Or a cure."

"Don't feel you need to," says Dad. "Don't feel you need to come back at all."

Is he telling me not to come back? I don't know how to re-spond. All I can focus on is a burning sensation in my chest. I want to cry, I want to yell, I want to hide in shame. But what he said makes it feel like he's the one abandoning me, not the other way around. So I refuse to back down.

"Fine," I say.

Prudence knocks on the door. "Helloooo? Shouldn't you be open by now?"

The day passes like any other work day, but Dad and I don't exchange a word. The bread is still baked to perfection, the customers bring energy and chatter, the winter sun peeks through the window until it begins to darken outside and we shut the store.

"I'll do apple turnovers and seedy loaves," I say to Dad as he flips the sign on the front door. "They're always a hit at the Harethorn markets."

Dad shrugs, not looking me in the eye.

I feel bad, but at the same time, I feel perfectly justified. I haven't really done anything wrong. I'm just living a life of my own.

The next day, I go to the stables to find a pack-horse that will be able to carry the bakery ingredients on the journey to Harethorn. I'll have to rely on a Harethorn baker letting me use their ovens – bringing 3-day-old apple turnovers from Schlafhold simply won't cut it.

At the stables is Haystack, shovelling horse manure in a brown stallion's stall. He took over his family's farm and stables last year, and they have flourished beyond expectation. Healthy, strong horses that breed yearly and produce hale foals.

He doesn't hear me approaching.

"Haystack!" I call.

He looks up quickly, surprised. His face breaks into a broad smile when he sees me.

"Minnow!" he says. "What's brought you here? After a horse?"

"Just need one for a week or so. I'm travelling to Harethorn and need someone to carry the packs."

Haystack nods. "Wave is probably the best choice." He leads me through the stables until we reach a medium-sized grey-white mare. She has heavily lidded eyes and appears to be completely unfazed by my presence.

"She'll do anything you ask of her," explains Haystack. "You gotta promise you'll bring her back. She's definitely my favourite here." He pats Wave on the rump.

"How's Helix?" I venture.

Haystack's expression turns dark. "Not good. He can't walk."

"That bad?"

"His whole leg's wrecked, Min," Haystack says. He's the only person besides Dad who gets away with calling me 'Min'.

"Wrecked?" I think back to the sickening sight of Helix's torn-up thigh.

Haystack shakes his head grimly. "He's lucky Heron was able to save his life at all. He's still staying at the apothecary.

Mostly better now, I think. Too scared to go outside, more than anything."

"You must've been pretty shocked, too," I say.

"Oh, you know me. I ain't frightened of nothing." He grins. We both know it's a lie. He won't go near cats since one scratched him when we were kids. He won't touch trees, either. Too likely there will be bugs under the bark.

Haystack rubs the back of his neck. "But yeah, it freaked me out real good. Never seen anything like it."

"What did it look like?" I ask.

Haystack gulps. "The stories don't lie. That's all I'll say." Haystack nods his head in the direction of the horse. "So, you're off on an adventure, then?"

"Going to run a bakery stall at the Harethorn markets."

Haystack nods. "You'd be good at that. I bet you'll sell out. People always like you."

"Yes, the bread usually turns out well enough, if I balance the ingredients right."

"I didn't mean the bread," says Haystack. He quickly looks away. "Never mind."

I run my hand across Wave's body. She feels so smooth.

"Is Cillian going with you?" Haystack asks, his voice quiet. I nod.

"That's good," says Haystack, although his tone is monotonous. "I've met him a few times now. He's smart, that fellow. Smart like you."

"Smart's not much use in Schlafhold," I chuckle. "Everyone here wants everything to stay the same. Plus, you're plenty smart. You can practically speak to these horses."

"I speak, for sure. Doesn't mean they talk back." He smiles. Then, he holds out his hand. Something is clenched in his fist. "You should take this."

He hands over a small wooden horse carved out of chestnut-coloured wood. Its body is frozen mid-gallop.

"Did you make this?" I marvel.

Haystack shakes his head. "Found it on the river bank one day. It brings good luck. Better luck than any horseshoe ever did."

"How do you know?"

"I have a good day whenever I'm carrying it. It sounds like you could use a few good days. Oh, I've got something else for you as well."

I follow him to the hut by the stables, where he lives with his parents and brother. I'm confused as to what Haystack could have for me, and why.

Haystack emerges a few moments later holding up a pair of brown trousers. "Your trousers look like they're about to fall to shreds. This is an extra pair of mine. Although they might be a bit too big for you, looking at them now." He holds them up.

"I can wear a belt," I assure him. "Thank you. It's hard finding clothing my size. And thanks for Wave. I'll take good care of her."

The last night before I leave, I check I've got everything I need for the journey. The baking basics: flour, yeast, oil, salt. Pumpkin and sunflower seeds for the seedy loaf. Apples, sugar and cinnamon for the turnovers. Next, some clothes from my generally almost-empty closet: a couple of long skirts, three blouses, my baker's apron, and Haystack's trousers. I have a hat as well, although most of the journey is under the shade of the forest. The hat still has old dried flowers threaded through it from when Thivya and I were children. Finally, I have a long black cloak that I can wrap around myself to keep warm in the darker stretches of the forest.

There's one more thing I have to do before I go.

"I'm going away for a bit, Ma," I say softly as I tuck a stray strand of hair behind her ear. "But I'll come back. I'm doing this to help you."

I stand up straight. I watch her for a few moments, remembering when I thought she'd called my name. It seems impossible now, watching how still she is and how unseeing her eyes seem. I notice her lips are dry, so I dampen a cloth and dab them.

I hear Dad approaching the doorway, stopping, and then retreating again. He doesn't want to see me. I'd hoped he might soften slightly and offer a farewell, but he keeps his distance. It stings.

I take a final look at Ma. I imagine her face lit up again, her playful smile, the wisdom in her eyes. I remember the way she moved around the house with such grace, almost dancing, and the way she would lean in towards Dad and kiss him on the cheek. I remember how she would always stoop slightly and face me when there was something important she had to tell me, placing a hand on each of my shoulders and looking deep into my eyes.

I know I'm making the right choice.

CHAPTER 8

The chilly morning fog threatens to seep through my blouse. I tug at my cloak so it covers my arms. Wave stands beside me, saddled with packs. We wait outside the bakery for Cillian.

To my surprise, Thivya strides up the street towards me and places her hands on her hips.

"I hear you're running away with some boy?" she asks pointedly.

I roll my eyes. "I'm going to Harethorn for a few days, and he happens to be coming too."

Thivya narrows her eyes. "Men are trouble, Minnow."

"The worst man I've ever met in Schlafhold is Smith, and he's not even that bad," I reply. "There are no evil villains like in fairy stories. Anyway, Cillian has proven himself to be a good friend."

"Just... keep your head," Thivya advises. "Don't get swept off your feet."

"I won't," I promise. "I'm not going because of Cillian. I've got a mission to complete."

Thivya nods, understanding. "Then I wish you all the best. Stay safe."

Cillian arrives, a pack slung over his shoulder. He smiles when his eyes meet mine.

"Are you ready?" he asks.

I nod.

We set off, following the path north of Schlafhold. Wave clops along contentedly. Cillian and I walk on either side of her.

"Cold today," Cillian observes.

"Yeah," I reply.

There's a silence. I suddenly worry that this is what the next three days is going to look like: us walking next to the horse in silence, occasionally commenting on the weather.

I try to think of something more interesting to talk about, but the effort of it is just making it even harder.

"So, Harethorn," Cillian begins.

I breathe a sigh of relief.

Cillian continues, "I've never properly visited. It sounds like you know a lot more about it. Please, enlighten me."

"Okay. I'll start with the boring elements. It's stood for over six hundred years, and it's home to at least a thousand people."

"Why not more? Surely it's a large city, if it's existed for that long?"

"It's not a city. Just a town. And no-one's interested in making it bigger. It's like Schlafhold: everyone's happy with things as they are."

"It sounds like a bit more happens in Harethorn compared to Schlafhold, though?"

"Yes. Unlike Schlafhold, Harethorn draws people in. They have several events a year. There's the Food Market Spectacular, which we'll be seeing. There's the boat races in spring. And there's the music fair every summer."

"Nothing in autumn, then?"

"The pumpkin festival. They see who's grown the biggest pumpkin. And then the judges decide which pumpkin is the best in every way."

"Not just the biggest?"

"No." I grin, remembering the assortment of pumpkins I saw the year I got to visit. "A pumpkin can be so many things. Different shapes, different colours, different textures. I saw one that looked like an hourglass."

Cillian raises his eyebrows.

"The people are a bit different in Harethorn, though," I explain. "A little less... relaxed. And when it's a festival or market day, there are people everywhere. Everyone is trying to get your attention and make you buy things. Even while you're working at your own stall!"

"What do you think my chances of someone selling me a Blessed orange are?"

"Hmm. Why would a fruit be Blessed in the first place?" I question.

"Perhaps someone asked a Witch to Bless their crop? So that their trees would produce ample fruit every year?"

"That seems the most likely explanation." I wonder what the cost would be for a Blessing like that.

We continue following the path until noon, which seems like a natural time to stop and rest. Cillian has brought sliced cheese to complement the bread I inevitably packed. We eat quickly, aware that we need to make it to the village of Byrne before nightfall. It's not that far, but I don't fancy spending any more time in this biting cold than I have to.

"So," says Cillian as we begin walking again. "I noticed you're close with that woman in the village? Thivya?"

I nod. "We've been friends since childhood."

"And those other boys were schooled at the same time – Smith, Helix and..."

"Haystack."

"That's right. An interesting nickname. Based on his shape?"

I cringe. "I don't remember. I hope not. I don't think I'd use it, if that was the case."

"Right. Were the boys kind, otherwise?"

I shrug. "Smith liked to put everyone down. He couldn't stand being outsmarted and could always find a way to insult you if your intelligence threatened his."

"Sounds like a real charmer."

"He's harmless, really. All bark and no bite. Then there's Helix. He doesn't seem to care much about anyone else. As for Haystack... He has a heart of gold. But he's too shy to really show it."

"Not a large pool of men to consider courting."

I blush. "There are a couple of other young men working on the farms, but I barely know them. The bakery keeps me so busy, I'll probably never have time to marry!" I let out a high-pitched laugh which instantly sounds forced.

"Do you want to?" asks Cillian.

"Are you asking me?" I say with a smirk, trying not to let out another embarrassing laugh.

He meets my gaze and doesn't say anything. His look is so serious, as if he's scrutinising me. My smile fades.

Finally, he looks back at the road ahead of us and begins walking at a faster pace. I don't know what I've done to cause his sobriety. I consider apologising, but don't want to rekindle a conversation that he would rather move on from.

I remember his difficult past with love. The woman he was close to for a single night. He never told me if he loved her. Is it possible to fall in love that quickly? Or was she just an incongruent heartbeat? I wonder if he asked her to stay after the child was born.

It only takes a few minutes before Cillian brightens up again and the conversation goes back to normal. But I feel like I've seen a more fragile part of him, something I need to be careful not to fish to the surface.

Byrne comes into view just as the sky begins to turn orange. Smoke rises from dozens of chimneys as villagers stave off the cold. Cillian and I head towards the inn, a ramshackle building with an old, broken, upturned horse-drawn cart out the front. A stable-boy obediently takes Wave around to the back of the building.

Just as I'm raising my knuckles to knock on the door to the inn, a frizzy-haired woman with a thoroughly freckled face opens it and looks me up and down.

"One room or two?" she barks bluntly, eyeing Cillian with something akin to suspicion.

"Two," Cillian and I say in unison. Thankfully.

The woman nods. "Good, good. We have ladies' quarters and men's rooms." She opens the door all the way and ushers us through.

"What's the difference?" I ask.

She looks at me incredulously, as if the question has never been asked before. "Men get larger rooms. Ladies get the nicer chamber pots."

The night passes without incident. Cillian and I have dinner in the downstairs area of the inn – a simple pairing of lamb and potatoes. After that, we retire to our separate rooms. I share my room with a woman named Chrys, who is visiting from Harethorn. She tells me about how she makes quilts and goes out to each village every few months to sell her work. I realise she made the bluebell-themed quilt that Betty keeps in her living room, and Chrys is thrilled to hear all about it.

Even though I spent plenty of time with Cillian today, I find myself missing him. His warm nature, his thoughtful conversation, his calm presence. And, for the first time in my life, I feel lonely in my own bed. Maybe it's because I'm not at home, where everything is close and familiar. But the thought of Cillian lying beside me with an arm holding me close makes me ache. I imagine the feeling of his chest as he breathes in and out. It comforts me and excites me at the same time.

Eventually I have to banish the thought from my mind. It's too distracting. I need to get a good night's sleep if I'm going to have energy for tomorrow's travels.

When we set out the next morning, Cillian looks a little worse for wear. His dark curls are a mess, suggesting a night of tossing and turning. He doesn't have bags under his eyes as such, but there are definitely lines where there aren't usually.

"How did you sleep?" I venture.

"The mattress was lumpy," Cillian responds. "The floor was more comfortable."

My Dad is usually grumpy after a night of poor sleep, but Cillian appears to be unchanged besides being slightly quieter. We take a longer lunch break. The village of Bellhope is only three hours' walk away by noon, so we don't rush.

I check that all of Wave's saddle packs are still holding strong – the last thing I need is for a punctured bag of flour to leave me with nothing left but a white trail behind me when I get to Harethorn.

Wanting to engage Cillian in conversation again, I ask, "What was Wrensaw like when you first got there?"

He tilts his head to the side a little as he thinks. "It was a lot of things. The edge of the forest was burnt, as were many of the buildings on the perimeter. There was lots of catapult damage, too. Rubble everywhere. They are a very resilient people, but most of them had lost friends and family during the raids. I admired their optimism when we started rebuilding."

"We were never affected by the War for the Wilds," I say. "A few people went off to fight. Everyone read the news and the missives. There were a couple of months without any of the fruits that grow up north. Don't get me wrong, everyone was extremely passionate about it all. Of course we wanted to pro-tect the Wilds and make sure the forest was never destroyed."

"Even if it meant letting the Twisteds keep surviving?"

I hesitate. "Dad and the others said that the enemy – the Urithians, that is – deliberately encouraged Twisteds to move towards towns and villages during the war, to scare people into siding with them."

Cillian narrows his eyes as he considers this. "But how would the Urithians orchestrate something like that? You can't reason with a Twisted. It's not like they talk. They attack on sight."

"I heard that there are things that can lure them. Whistling sounds that mimic their calls to each other. Raw meat and bones. And they hate the smell of burning mugwort."

"Maybe we should pick up some mugwort in Harethorn and take it back with us," muses Cillian. "I could use it at Haunted Lake."

"I don't know if it's true," I admit. "Sometimes, stories in the village have been retold so many times that there's nothing left of the original."

The path curves left towards Bellhope. The village looks very different to Byrne and Schlafhold. Bellhope is built over a series of hills, with most of the forest cleared to make way for farms. Many of the buildings are homesteads shared between several families.

I know of a nice inn at the close edge of the village, and I lead Cillian and Wave to its doors. The inn was once a huge barn, but it has been converted into a well-kept abode for trav-ellers.

It's the kind of place you walk inside and up to the counter before ordering a drink and booking a room. I leave Wave by the entrance, and then Cillian and I make our way inside the inn.

The room is buzzing with red-faced men – and a couple of women – slurping ales and cheering at card games. The heat of the place is overwhelming, so I quickly take my cloak off. Despite the discomfort, I have to admit it's nice to be fully warm for the first time in ages.

A muscly man with long blonde hair stands at the counter, drying recently washed ale mugs. He doesn't look up as we approach.

"Yep?" he says.

"I was hoping we might be able to book two rooms for tonight, please."

The bartender shakes his head. "Not possible, I'm afraid. We've got a full house."

My mouth drops open. I wasn't prepared for this. It's another whole day of walking to get to Harethorn, and I don't fancy doing it overnight.

"Is there anywhere else in the village we could stay?" I ask.

The bartender shrugs. He puts down the ale mug and picks up another, starting the drying process once more. "The Lilly family always welcomes visitors, if you don't mind sharing with a couple of their eight children and four dogs."

"That... doesn't sound ideal," I say. I look questioningly at Cillian. He looks even more tired than this morning and starts rubbing his right eye.

"Thanks anyway," I say to the bartender. "I'm sure we can find shelter somewhere."

"We do have the Badger Room free," mentions the bartender.

"What? Why didn't you say that?"

"Well you asked for two rooms. I can only offer you the one. With one bed."

I look at Cillian. He's almost asleep standing up.

I nudge him with my elbow. "Hey. One room. One bed." I try to sound as blasé about it as possible.

"I can sleep on the floor," Cillian mutters.

"It's a pretty small place," discloses the bartender. "You could probably fit a thin mat alongside the bed."

"Thank you, that'll be just fine," I say. It beats snuggling up with the Lilly family's dogs. And... I'll get to be close to Cillian. Overnight. Just inches away from him, by the sound of things. Oh no, what if I snore? What if I talk in my sleep and keep him awake all night? Although looking at him now, I can't imagine anything will keep him awake.

When the bartender has finished with the ale mugs, he leads us upstairs to a tiny room at the end of a corridor. It looks like a space that was simply left over when the rest of the building was complete. The ceiling is slanted and the room has a tall, thin window that looks more like a repurposed crack between two wall panels.

"I'll grab a mat," says the bartender, stepping away.

I turn to Cillian. "I'll sleep on the mat. You deserve a bed tonight. You're in dire need of a proper sleep."

"Don't be ridiculous. I could never sleep on a bed and force a woman to sleep on the floor."

"And what exactly is it about being a woman that makes me unable to manage sleeping in slightly less than favourable conditions? Or is it that as a woman I don't get to make my own choice as to where I sleep?"

Cillian winces and sits on the edge of the bed. "Minnow, I'm too tired for this."

"Exactly. Get in the bed and get some sleep. I'll bring up something to eat."

CHAPTER 9

Cillian is fast asleep on the bed when I return to the room with two bowls of pottage. I fill my own stomach and leave his serving sitting in the corner. It's getting late, so I begin to prepare for bed. Unfortunately, there was no mat to be found in the inn. I've resigned myself to sleeping on the wooden floor.

As I'm about to lie down, Cillian reaches out and softly holds my wrist. His hand is so warm: he's been holding it curled up to his chest.

"Minnow," he whispers.

"What? You should be sleeping."

"Don't sleep on the floor."

"It's no bother. It's just for one night."

"There's room up here."

There is a moment of heavy silence.

I feel like I can't take full breaths. Oh no, I'm not having an episode of breathlessness, am I? This would be a terrible time. But no, this is something different. It's nervousness and excitement pinching at me. Last night I was wishing I could share a bed with Cillian. Now it could be a reality.

I look at the bed. I'll take up twice as much space as him. Will it bother him?

"Are you sure?" I ask.

"I'm sure." He shuffles backwards and pats the bed.

I climb in and absorb the warmth beneath me.

He props himself up onto his elbow and smiles at me as I roll onto my side and face him. Should I be facing him?

I've never seen him up this close. He has a tiny freckle above his right eyebrow that I haven't noticed before.

Cillian reaches out his hand and moves my hair away from my face.

My heart rate quickens. His skin doesn't touch mine.

"You're not like anyone else I've ever met," says Cillian, looking into my eyes.

"In a good way or a bad way?"

He chuckles. "In a good way. A very good way."

"And what do you mean by that?"

He takes my hand. Warm against my cool.

"You're so sweet and determined at the same time. Gentle but fierce," he states.

"I am *not* fierce," I counter.

"I think there's ferocity in you. I saw it in Walnut Woods. You were ready to fight to defend me. You're full of kindness, too. That's what I like most of all. You're travelling for days in the hope that you might just be able to find something to help your mother. You ran to Heron straightaway when Helix was injured. And you work six days a week at the bakery to support your dad."

"I don't just do that out of *kindness*," I argue.

"What is it, then? Loyalty? Love of the work?"

"All of the above, I guess."

"There's something on top of all that I've noticed, too," observes Cillian.

"Oh? What's that?"

"You're beautiful."

I don't know how to respond. Deny it? I don't want to seem self-deprecating. Agree? Then I'm egotistical. Tell him that I think he's beautiful, too? I wouldn't be lying. Or I could just say 'thank you' and take the compliment.

As a result of being lost in my thoughts, I have just been staring wordlessly and expressionlessly at Cillian. He tilts his head slightly, as if silently assessing whether I'm okay.

"I..." I stammer, "That's... a lovely thing to say."

"I mean it." He lowers himself onto the pillow and shuffles closer to me.

My gaze flickers down to his lips. Forget everything else, I actually want to kiss him. I've never kissed a man before, but I want to kiss Cillian Gray more than anything else right now.

"Minnow," he says softly.

"Yes, Cillian?"

"If it wasn't for my past – and the Curse – then I would really like to..." His voice trails away.

I wait for him to finish his sentence, but he doesn't say anything else.

"Cillian?" I prompt.

He presses his lips together and shakes his head. "It doesn't matter."

He rolls onto his back.

I feel as if I'm a candle that's been blown out. No, that's not right. I feel like a campfire that's been doused by water. Or a forest fire drowned out by rain. I want to reach out to him, to place my fingertips on his arm and ask him to tell me more, but I don't want him to withdraw further.

I roll onto my back and try not to let out the massive sigh brewing inside me. I shouldn't have gotten myself so excited about what was nothing more than a brief moment where we lay facing each other with our lips a few inches apart. Nothing more than that. Although a slight tingle between my legs suggests I got quite a bit excited.

This is all new territory for me. Overwhelmed by it all and knowing that nothing else is going to happen tonight, I roll onto my side facing away from Cillian.

"Goodnight," I say.

"Sleep well, Minnow." I hear rustling as he rolls onto his side, facing away.

I can feel the warmth emanating from his body, even though he is facing the other direction. Our backs are almost touching. Surely, at some point in the night, one of us will lean in towards the other during our sleep? Or roll over? What happens then?

I close my eyes. It doesn't take long for the exhaustion of today's travel to settle and bring me to the point of sleep.

Morning light trickles in through the so-called 'window' slit in the wall. My eyes are crusty with sleep, so I rub them with my knuckles until my eye sockets feel weird. Cillian shifts behind me, his back still facing me. I slowly sit up and pull on my cloak to ward off the morning chill.

I stand in front of the thin ray of light, letting the gentle warmth of the sun heat one side of my face. I watch Cillian as he begins to stir from sleep. I realise that despite his straight posture and easy manner in day-to-day life, there is a weight hanging over him that is absent in the innocence of sleep. The Curse can't touch him in the quiet realm of the unconscious.

Our breakfast is rushed – we need to travel quickly if we are to make it to Harethorn before nightfall. Then, we need a good night's sleep to ensure we have the energy needed for the big day tomorrow.

Everything is normal between Cillian and I today, thankfully. I was worried our out-of-the-ordinary exchange last night would create an awkwardness, but he acts as if nothing has changed. This mostly fills me with relief, although part of me wants to stoke the fire again. He called me beautiful. We lay so close to each other... my heart leaps. Okay, now is not the time.

As we get closer to Harethorn, more people become visible on the road. I assume they are all travelling for the markets. Some of them pull along big carts full of goods – everything from pottery to vegetables to (very odorous) fresh fish.

Cillian eyes a cart carrying crates of fruit. I stand on tiptoe as we get closer and see there is a crate full of oranges.

Cillian walks up to the owner of the cart and strikes up a conversation. "Your fruits look exceptional. May I ask where they are from?"

"I grew them myself in Fairmark. There are many orchards and trees there. These aren't mine alone – I am here representing everyone in the village. We always work together."

"It sounds like a pleasant place to live, if that is your way of life." Cillian returns to my side and shakes his head. "I don't think he has what we need."

I keep my eye out for anyone who looks like a healer of some sort, but something tells me that the man I am looking for has already reached Harethorn. As the road becomes busier and we draw closer to other travellers, I hear snatches of conversations that assure me I will find what I seek.

"He washed clean a woman with pox and she was completely healed," says one woman.

"I heard all he needs to do is poke people in the right spots to bring them back from the edge of death," says another.

I realise I never learnt the name of this mysterious healer, so I pipe up, "Excuse me, may I ask who it is that you speak of?"

"A famed healer by the name of Autumn Carraway. He is conducting a public healing tomorrow in the town square. I'm hoping he can cure my skin condition. I've had it since I was a child." The woman holds out her arms, which are pink and scaly. She continues, "Apparently he will only be there for two hours, though. Then he is off to the next place. All those big cities."

Two hours? I glance around at the people around us. How many of them have come to see Autumn Carraway? How will I get a moment of his time? I don't even have my Ma with me. Plus, I'll be working at the bakery stall most of the day. Maybe I can find him afterwards, when he's packing up from the show. Perhaps he likes apple turnovers? I could find a dairy stall beforehand and serve him one with whipped cream. Hmm. It is unlikely his feelings towards baked goods are equivalent to mine. I'll have to think of some other bartering chip.

Cillian hasn't spoken for a while. I imagine he is growing anxious about not finding what he needs. I notice him grinding his teeth.

I place a comforting hand on his bicep. "It's okay. We don't have to worry about these things until tomorrow."

"But how will I know?" Cillian mutters. "What does a Blessed orange even look like? It's not like it will glow."

"Maybe it's something you just feel." I hesitate. "The way you feel your Curse."

He casts me a sideways glance. He's clearly doubtful as to whether I have any clue what it's like living with a Curse. To be fair, I don't. But I know he can feel it.

CHAPTER 10

"Welcome to Harethorn," announces a tall man wearing a top hat as we arrive at the gate to the town. Harethorn is the only place I've been to that has a gate. All of the villages just let you wander right in, and often don't have any kind of outer wall at all.

"I'll need to see everyone's papers before we let you through."

A murmur passes through the crowd of travellers. Cillian and I exchange shocked glances. Papers? What papers?

"Only joking!" the tall man calls out. "Everyone is welcome here."

I breathe a sigh of relief. We are let through the gate. The aged streets and buildings of Harethorn come into view. Lamps on either side of the road light up a path for travellers with carts. Townsfolk mill about, some purchasing dinner from street vendors, others closing up their main street shops for the day. One man stands on a corner playing the flute. It reminds me of Helix, and I mentally send him well wishes.

Our inn tonight is full to the brim, but the innkeepers were prepared and have ensured there is room for all. It's a relief, because I'm not sure whether I would have wanted to share a bed with Cillian again. I mean, I definitely do. But not if it's going to end up like last time. He's grown increasingly concerned about the Blessed orange, despite my assurances that if there's one anywhere in the world, it'll be in Harethorn tomorrow.

In my dormitory are a group of dancers who are scheduled to perform a traditional dance in the afternoon tomorrow. They chatter animatedly and brush each other's hair. It reminds me of brushing Ma's hair, which I would usually be doing around this time. I stave off the oncoming feelings of guilt about Dad by remembering that the whole reason I'm here is to help Ma. I take a deep breath. I *will* succeed and get what I need from Autumn Carraway. I have to.

"It was a close call," I overhear one of the dancers saying as she weaves her friend's hair into a tight braid.

Another dancer pipes up, "They took her right to the edge of the bay before the sheriff showed up. Even then, it took a group of townsfolk to intervene before they would let her go. Then they just sailed away before they could face any consequences."

One of the dancers notices my confused expression. "We're talking about the dancer who almost got taken last year."

"Taken?"

"Yes. Sometimes, pirates park their boats on the river, disguised as merchant vessels. Really, they're here to recruit people to work on their boats. And when they can't recruit, they kidnap. That's what happened to my cousin, Emili," explains a woman with fuzzy black hair and a sparkle in her eyes. "Thankfully, the pirates were intercepted by the authorities."

I wonder if there are any other sinister threats in Harethorn I haven't considered. Of course, Dad would only ever have shown me the best parts of town. At least I'm not a beautiful dancer – that might work in my favour.

A true baker, I get up hours before dawn and lead Wave through the streets to the nearest bakery. I remember it clearly from the last few times I visited the town with Dad. It's run by a ruddy-faced, heavyset man named Grieg, who specialises in cakes and pastries. He has always been very welcoming towards Dad and I; although, on those occasions, Dad had sent word weeks in advance informing of our arrival. I don't know how Grieg will feel about me popping in unannounced on the morning of the markets.

I tap the wooden door to the bakery gently, hoping that I'm not too early. Thankfully, Grieg opens it straightaway. He squints at me, clearly seeing I'm a familiar face but not being able to place me. Finally, he smiles.

"Perry's daughter, right?"

I nod.

His eyes widen. "He's not here? He's not... you know, passed, has he?"

I shake my head and attempt a reassuring smile. "He's well."

Grieg beckons me inside. There's a row of cupcakes on the bench, iced with cherries on top.

"So, what's brought you here? I didn't hear anything from you two about having a market stall."

I shift uncomfortably from one foot to the other. "We weren't planning on it." How much do I tell him? "I had to come to Harethorn for something else. But I might need money. So I brought ingredients for bread and apple turnovers. And I was wondering..."

He raises an eyebrow expectantly.

"...I was wondering if I could please use your ovens." The words spill out in a hurry.

I can see Grieg hesitating. A muscle near the side of his eye twitches.

"I'll give you ten percent of any profits," I jump in.

"Twen-..." Grieg begins, but then he lets out a sigh. "Ten sounds fine."

I think he pities me, or at least doesn't want to take advantage of someone so young. He still sees me as Perry's daughter.

Cillian seeks me out once the sun has risen, following the scent of freshly-baked bread.

"I've finished the apple turnovers and just have three seedy loaves to go," I inform him. "Grieg has a spare wooden table we can set up down the street. Can you take it as close to the square as possible? Hopefully we can get a clear view of Autumn Carraway."

Cillian nods and lugs the table out the door. I check on the seedy loaves and realise with a fright that they are on the cusp of burning. Grieg's ovens get hotter more quickly than Dad's. I remove them and lay them out on the bench next to the other loaves and the turnovers. There's not as much as I'd imagined. I doubt any profits will be enough to convince Autumn Carraway to visit Schlafhold. So, my hope rests in either a portable cure or my powers of persuasion.

As soon as I step outside the bakery to transport my goods in a cart down the street, I am overwhelmed by how busy it is. The markets are always an overstimulating experience. People lead animals through the streets while others heckle at them to keep the animals away from their stalls. Huge tubs of fruit and vegetables are laid out and observed by ever-vigilant stall-holders. Folks dressed in wealthier bright colours and fabrics mingle with those in plain browns. The smells of foreign perfumes and fresh fish taint the air with every awakening of a breeze. Gulls perch on nearby rooftops, keeping watch for any dropped scraps they can swoop down and seize.

Once, it would have intimidated me. Today, it's wonderful.

I go past a stall with an assortment of rare teas on offer, and remind myself to visit later to try and get a free sample. I can smell the cinnamon and cardamom from here. Mingled with it is the smell of mugwort from the next stall, which appears to sell nothing but bushels of the green plant.

Cillian has set up our table not too far from the town square. If we crane our necks, we will be able to see the podium where Autumn Carraway is set to appear. I start laying out the baked goods. In less than half an hour I've already pocketed a quarter of what I'd hoped to earn today. Most people are friendly, but some are evidently here to pass through and engage with the vendors as little as possible.

One middle-aged man approaches the table before midday and is clearly the more friendly type. He wears a dark blue scarf and a lime green cap decorated with buttons of different shapes and colours. "Good morning. May I ask what those delectable-looking pastries are?"

"Those are apple turnovers, and these are loaves of seedy bread."

"Any chance I could sample one?" he asks.
"I can't really cut open the turnovers," I apologise. "But you can have a slice of the bread." I cut a slice and hand it to him.

He bites a corner and his eyes light up with delight. "This really is something," he commends through a half-chewed mouthful. "And – forgive me for asking – but was it your husband who baked this?" He nods towards Cillian, who is wrapping up a loaf for another customer.

I laugh, despite feeling somewhat offended. "No, I'm the baker," I explain. "He's just helping out. And he's not my husband."

"I see," says the man, with a nod of his head. He looks pensively into the distance for a moment, then returns his attention to me. He takes out his protection knife, which has a slightly curved blade and a black hilt. Its simplicity reminds me of Dad's. "I'm Fraser," he says. "I'm here with a group of travelling vendors, although I feel they resent me for my general lack of skills and the fact I don't actually have anything to sell. I'm hoping that bringing back some of these loaves and half a dozen apple turnovers will redeem me in their eyes, at least a little bit."

I beam and draw my own protection knife, hilt facing him. "My name's Minnow. I'd be delighted to sell you as many as you'd like."

It turns out he would like a *lot*. Seven loaves and six turnovers.

"This should keep you and your fellows fed for a while," I remark.

"I hope so. We've got a big crew, though."

"Oh, are you travelling by boat? Where are you headed next?"

"We will be sailing north this evening as soon as the markets are over. I love taking off in the twilight. It feels like the perfect time to start an adventure."

"I'm more of a morning person, myself. But all bakers are."

He struggles to gather up his purchases in one go. I offer to load them onto Wave and walk to his boat with him, but he politely declines.

"I'll fetch a cart," he insists, and returns a couple of minutes later with a borrowed wheelbarrow.

"Here's a little bonus," he says, pressing an extra couple of silver coins into my hand.

"Oh, that's really unnecessary," I begin, but he shakes his head.

"You've been a wonderful help," Fraser says, "And you clearly have a gift. I hope you keep using it."

I smile again. "Thank you, Fraser." I wave to him as he disappears into the crowd.

The bell in the big clock in the town square starts to ring out. *Clang, clang.* Twelve times. It's midday. Autumn Carraway is here.

CHAPTER 11

The town square quickly fills up with desperate people shoving each other to get to the podium at the front. Our stall isn't in the perfect spot to view the podium, but I can catch glimpses between the amassed bodies.

A smiley, stout woman steps up and addresses the crowd. "As the mayor of Harethorn, it is my pleasure to welcome our most esteemed of guests, Autumn Carraway."

An old man steps up to the podium with the aid of a helping hand from the mayor. And when I say old, I mean *old*. His face is lined and wizened, and his head is bald besides a few errant tufts of white hair. So many things about him seem sharp: his pointed nose, his knobbly elbows, his triangular chin. But when I stand on tiptoe and get a good look at his face, I can see that his green eyes are also sharp – he has a very keen mind.

"Give the man some space!" instructs the mayor as the crowd surges forwards.

"I don't have much time today," croaks Carraway. "I will likely not be able to treat all of you. Since there are so many, I will be selecting from the crowd at random, with the aid of my servant, Betta. Bear in mind, I must prioritise those who can pay for my services."

The first person brought up is a man who has had a painful limp for the past year. Carraway instructs him to lie on his stomach, and he obeys. Carraway kneels beside him and places his hands on his lower back. A mighty *crack!* rings out as Carraway presses into it. He repeats this a few times, adjusting his position slightly each time. Finally, he steps back. "Rise."

The man gets to his feet. He stumbles a little, and the audience members hold their breath as they wonder if the limp remains. The man stretches out his leg and takes a few unsteady steps. Then, he turns to Carraway with a look of elation. "I'm mended. You've healed me! There is no more pain."

Carraway places a comforting hand on his shoulder. "You are welcome, friend."

The healed man holds out his coin purse to Carraway. "Take it. All of it."

Carraway peers into the coin purse. "This will do. Thank you."

Next up is a woman I recognise from the journey – the one with the scaly skin. Carraway inspects her arms closely, holding them gently up to the light.

He steps back. "There is a plant that can help you, but it is rare and I only have one to give. How important is this cure to you?"

The woman's mouth drops open as she considers this. Finally: "This is all I've wanted for decades."

Carraway nods slowly. "Since it's the only plant, it will cost you one gold coin."

There are a few gasps in the crowd. One gold coin is the equivalent of one hundred silver coins. I look down at my earnings for the day and add it to the savings I've brought with me. I only have forty-four silver coins in my possession.

The unrest amongst the crowd indicates that others were not anticipating such steep fees either.

The woman at the podium looks down. "I have only brought eighty-five silver coins."

Carraway presses his lips together. He turns to the crowd. "Is there anyone else here in need of treatment for the same condition and able to pay the cost of one gold coin?"

Someone raises their hand.

Carraway turns back to the woman. "I am sorry, but I am unable to help you today."

The woman bursts into tears. Betta, Carraway's servant, guides her away.

I feel something sink inside me. What if I can't afford the cure for Ma? That could be even worse than finding out there is no cure at all – knowing that it was my fault for failing, for not doing enough.

Carraway continues assessing people's various ailments and offering treatments. Sometimes these are ointments or consumables, and sometimes they involve him laying hands on them and manipulating their bodies. Occasionally, sickening cracking sounds ring out and I expect cries of agony and broken bones, but the patient will rise up and declare that their pain has gone at last.

I can't see the clock from my position, but I follow the path of the sun in the sky and determine that it is just past one-thirty. We've sold out, so we start packing up. Cillian offers to take the table and cart back to Grieg's bakery. I hand him a few silver coins to pass on to Grieg.

"I'll stop by all the fruit stalls on the way back," he explains. "I imagine I'll have to listen to a fair few stories about how each seller's fruits were grown and why theirs are the best in the land. Will you be okay on your own?"

"Of course," I reply.

Once Cillian has gone, I weave my way through the crowd to get closer to the front. I receive a few disapproving glares from people as I push past, but I know I need to be closer if I stand any chance of Carraway noticing me.

"Who's next?" Carraway calls to the crowd.

I shoot my hand into the air. Carraway doesn't even look at me, and instead beckons towards a dainty-looking woman wearing a large hat.

Someone sidles up to me and I flinch, not expecting them to get so close.

I realise it is Betta, Autumn Carraway's wiry assistant.

"I might be able to get you up there," he states. "Tell me in twenty words what you need help with."

"My Ma hasn't spoken for five years. It's like she's not fully awake, even when she's up. Does it have to be exactly twen-..."

Betta interrupts me. "And where is your Ma?" He looks past me.

I deflate a little. "She's back home in Schlafhold."

"How do you expect Autumn Carraway to help your Ma if she's not even here?!" His tone is demeaning, and he looks down at me as if I am a child.

My voice rises in pitch as I try to defend myself. "I thought he might have a cure I could take home to her. Or even some advice. Or maybe he would even be willing to travel…"

Betta shakes his head and utters a small laugh. "Autumn Carraway does not make house calls, especially not to tiny villages in the middle of nowhere. Do you really think that would be worth his precious time? Go." He shoos me away with a flick of his hand. He starts to walk away.

"If you would just let me speak to him-…" I attempt, grabbing onto the end of Betta's sleeve.

He shakes me off. "I said go. Be on your way, or I will call the town guards."

I linger at the edge of the town square and watch until the end of Carraway's healing demonstration. A man with lice is drenched in a pungent liquid. A lump on a woman's foot is burnt away. A half-blind man is given a special circle of glass and sees perfectly when looking through it. A person's loose-hanging shoulder is shoved back into place.

"Heron could have managed that one," I mumble.

Finally, Autumn Carraway straightens up, alone on the podium. "Thank you all for your attendance today. For those of you who have been healed: go now and enjoy your lives to the fullest. Relish every moment. And for those of you I could not serve today, I offer my deepest condolences. Do not envy or resent your fellows who were able to receive my assistance. Your time may come, for I intend to travel these lands again. Healing is my craft, and those who damage my handiwork will not be favoured in my eyes."

He steps down from the podium and is ushered away by Betta and a couple of town guards before anyone can reach out for him.

This could be my chance. I take a deep breath, ready to race forwards and get Carraway's attention before he disappears completely.

Just as I take a step, I feel fingernails digging deep into my arms and holding me back. Someone is grabbing me from behind. My first thought is that Cillian has returned and is guiding me away. But the nails dig in deep and I'm pushed roughly towards the edge of the crowd.

"Ow!" I cry out, attempting to pull free.

One hand lets go of me, but I feel the tip of a knife press into my lower back.

"Walk where I tell you," says a voice in my ear. It takes me a moment to recognise it.

Fraser.

CHAPTER 12

"**D**own there."

I hesitate as I behold the secluded alleyway in front of me. One could barely even call it that – it's a narrow gap between rows of tall buildings.

I shake my head, even though I know I don't have a choice.

I feel Fraser's blade digging slightly deeper into my back. It hasn't cut me yet.

My own knife is in the front pocket of my apron, but I doubt I could take it out and fight him off. I have to play along for now.

I startle as a man steps out from the shadows ahead of me. He is average height, with dark eyes and hair. His beard is short but messy.

He looks me up and down, appraising me. "This her, then?" he says, chewing something at the same time. He has a silky accent I am unfamiliar with.

"Obviously," responds Fraser behind me. "Who else?"

The stranger takes a few steps, covering the remaining distance between us. Something about the way he moves reminds me of a cat.

He places his index finger underneath my chin. "And did the baker put up a fight?"

I turn my head away and he withdraws his hand.

"I see she doesn't like us yet," observes the stranger.

"She came along easily enough," says Fraser.

The stranger smiles at me. "Good girl." He flicks his attention back to Fraser. "She will do." He beckons to me. "Come along."

"I'm not going anywhere with you. I don't even know who you are."

The stranger rolls his eyes. "You will find out once we're aboard the ship. You'll learn everything you need to know there. Now, we need to get going."

I don't budge, so Fraser shoves me forwards and I stumble a few paces.

I use the opportunity to grab my protection knife from my apron pocket. I spin around and strike blindly in Fraser's direction.

The blade catches slightly as it slices his forearm, ripping through the fabric of his sleeve.

"Argh!" he cries out, instinctively stepping back.

I hear a shuffle behind me and know that the stranger is drawing his own knife. I turn around to face him.

He twirls his knife around in his hand, dancing the hilt between his fingers. Instantly, I know I am no match for him.

All the pieces are falling into place now. There's a ship, and they want me on board. They're pirates, and I'm being 're-cruited'.

The stranger closes in. Soon, I'm backed against a wall.

Fraser hisses sharply. He wraps his scarf around his arm to stem the bleeding and shoots me an angry glare.

"Come quietly with us, now," says the stranger.

I hold my knife out in front of me. "No."

The stranger glances at Fraser. "Do you have the sack?"

Fraser nods.

The stranger pockets his knife. In a swift movement, he steps forwards and slams his hand down on the bone of my forearm, causing me to drop my knife in shock. Pain shoots through my arm. I gasp.

Before I have a chance to react further, a black fabric sack is pulled over my head. My wrists are seized and tied behind my back. The thin rope is wound tight, and already I know that there are red marks forming on my skin beneath it.

I feel the hood of my cloak being lifted and draped over my head. An arm wraps around my shoulders and begins guiding me forwards.

Blinded and bound, I don't struggle. I know I'm at the mercy of two men: one skilled in combat, and the other pissed off at me for cutting his arm.

We continue down the alleyway.

"Our baker died of completely natural causes," explains the stranger, talking as if we are having a casual conversation at the dinner table. "We were worried we wouldn't find anyone good enough to replace him."

The sounds of chatter grow louder. We're approaching a street. I realise that to anyone passing by, I just look like an ordinary person hiding their face under a cloak. Another sound begins to reach my ears: the rush of the river. This is followed by the calls of people working on the docks and the creaking of wooden boats. A gull cries out. Once, I would have enjoyed the sounds. Now, every second fills me with fear. I'll be trapped. I'll never go home again. I'll never see Ma, or Dad, or Cillian, or anyone else from the village. Instead, I'll be slaving away on a foul-smelling boat, surrounded by pirates who have no qualms when it comes to kidnapping, plundering and killing. What will they do to me if they don't like my cooking? There isn't much else I can offer...

I try to think about something else. Have I given up on a plan to escape? I could try to break free and make a run for it, I suppose. But my hands are bound and I won't be able to see a thing. Are there still townsfolk around who might notice and help me?

The ground beneath me changes in texture. Firm wooden slats. I must be walking onto a pier.

"Excuse me, miss, I think you dropped something," comes a male voice from behind me, barely audible through the fabric and cloak covering my ears.

"She hasn't dropped anything. You're mistaken," I hear Fraser say.

"No, I'm pretty sure she has. As far as I know, this is the only protection knife out there with a picture of her mother on it."

It's Cillian. Of course.

But he doesn't know how dangerous these men are.

The grip around my shoulders tightens. There is a heavy pause, like the earth's breath before a thunderstorm.

"I'll take her on board," comes the stranger's voice at last. "You deal with him."

"But my arm!" protests Fraser.

I feel the stranger pushing Fraser away from me and grabbing my shoulder roughly. He forces me forwards. I stumble but keep walking.

I hear Fraser drawing his protection knife behind me. I wish I could hear better and know what Cillian is doing. I wish I could see!

Instead, the main thing I can sense is the stranger gripping my shoulder as we turn left.

"A little ramp," he murmurs. I still don't manage to fully brace myself for the incline, and I fall forwards. Since my hands are bound, I can't put them out in front of me to stop the fall. My body hits the wood. The wood wobbles. That worries me.

"Ugh," sneers the stranger. He kicks my thigh with the tip of his boot. "Get up."

"How do you expect me to get up when I'm tied up like this?" I demand, but I can hear how muffled and quiet my voice is.

He bends down next to me and tries to slip his arm under the front of my body, curling around my waist. But I'm too heavy for him to lift.

Suddenly, he's pulling off the hood of the cloak and the dark sack covering my face. He holds the tip of his knife up to my cheek.

"No funny business," he says. "Straight up the ramp and onto the boat. Step out of line once and I'll scar that pretty face forever, and I'll personally make sure that boy back there becomes another body lost in the river." He reaches under my cloak and unties the rope around my wrists.

I climb to my feet and rub at the red impressions in my skin. I look up and see that we're at the top of a ramp leading onto a small ship. It looks unremarkable: it's designed to blend in.

I look back over my shoulder to see what Cillian is doing, but my view is blocked by the stranger.

"I said straight up the ramp."

I do as he says and find myself on the deck of the boat. The floor beneath me trembles slightly with the pulse of the river. A few crew members mill about, preparing for departure, clearly unfazed by my appearance. One man carries a box of vegetables from the deck and through a doorway into the depths below. I wonder if he stole them.

"This way," directs the stranger. He nudges me in the same direction, towards the doorway which I imagine leads to a steep staircase and, eventually, the galley. The dark, smelly galley where I am destined to live out the rest of my days.

Just as we reach the doorway, the crew member re-emerges. He offers me a quick, innocent smile and nods respectfully at the stranger.

The stranger places a hand on the crew member's chest, stopping him. "Did you get them?"

"Yes, of course," replies the crew member.

"And you're sure they're the right ones?" continues the stranger. "Those ones we bought last time rotted. I'm not dealing with another outbreak of scurvy."

"I was assured they are a special type which will last at least two years."

The stranger nods his head. "Good. And they're below deck?"

"They're in that box over there. I'll bring them down next."

I look to where the crew member is pointing. It's a wooden crate filled to the brim with oranges.

Oranges which, from what I've just heard, won't rot for years. Impossible, unless they are... Blessed.

The stranger whistles loudly, and the whole crew turn their attention to him. "Time to set sail, lads!"

As some ropes are pulled and others untied, the ship begins to come loose from the pier and give in to the pull of the river.

If I wait any longer, it will be too late.

I twist away from the stranger and start sprinting.

"Stop her!" yells the stranger.

I charge towards the unfortunate crew member holding the crate of oranges. He drops it in surprise, causing it to tip over. Perfectly round oranges spill everywhere. I scoop one up and shove it into my apron pocket as I race across the deck in the direction of the shore.

A small stretch of water is between the edge of the boat and the muddy shore. I don't have time to hesitate.

I leap straight over the edge and plummet towards the water. It hurts to break the surface. The water is numbingly cold.

It takes all of my effort to tread water and not get swept away by the river. I struggle to propel my body to the shore.

"Cillian!" I cry out in blind hope that he might be nearby.

"That's it!" I hear a voice respond, but it's not Cillian. It's the stranger aboard the ship.

I pivot around and see the stranger toss the end of a rope ladder over the edge of the boat.

"I'm not coming back!" I say, barely avoiding getting water in my mouth.

The stranger grins. "That's right. I'll make sure of that. You're far too much trouble."

He starts descending the ladder. I realise with horror that he is holding a longsword. I desperately reach for the shoreline, willing myself forwards with everything I have. I can hear the stranger splashing behind me. No doubt he is used to doing all kinds of things in the water… including killing.

The water becomes shallower. I try to dig my feet into the mud and then spring forwards.

"Minnow! Minnow, I'm here! Take my hand!" Cillian is on his knees on the riverbank, reaching out to me.

I reach my arm out, but take a final look behind me as I do.

The stranger is raising his sword, ready to bring it down over me…

Cillian dives into the water and rushes towards the stranger, jamming his knife into the stranger's shoulder. The stranger shrieks in pain and drops his sword, which sinks through the gloom to the river floor.

Cillian pulls out his bloodied knife and backs away, resisting the pull of the river.

The stranger caresses his own shoulder and his face wrinkles in pain. "How dare you! Do you know who I am?"

"No," Cillian and I say in unison.

"I'm-…" The stranger's voice becomes garbled as a wave of water invades his mouth.

I feel a tug on my sleeve. Cillian is already making his way back to the river bank. I quickly follow suit.

I am utterly exhausted when I pull myself out of the river. It's like being a shell with the insides sucked out of me. I lie on my back for a moment and notice the soft white clouds moving overhead. That one looks like an anvil. And that one looks like a loaf of bread. In fact, a lot of them look like loaves of bread…

"We have to get up," Cillian hisses.

I rise onto my elbows. "I'm so tired."

"I just knocked one person out and stabbed another," says Cillian. "I doubt the town guards will sit down and hear me out before arresting me and locking me up."

I get to my feet. Cillian looks at me, his black curls flattened on his head like an over-watered plant.

When his eyes meet mine, he softens. Suddenly, he pulls me into a tight hug, with one hand around my back and the other on the back of my head.

"I'm so glad you're safe," he whispers.

I melt into his embrace. But it only lasts for a few seconds, because then he's letting go and taking my hand, and we're hurrying to fetch Wave and make it to the edge of town.

Once we've made it through the gate and reached the cover of the forest, we stop to gather our breath. Cillian leans back against a tree trunk, letting out a deep huff of air. I wipe sweat from my brow.

"I have something for you," he says at last. From under his cloak, he produces my protection knife.

I take it. "Thank you. Thank you for saving it. And me. I have something for you as well."

I pull the perfect orange out of my apron pocket and hand it to Cillian. He holds it up to the light and marvels at it.

"A Blessed orange," he whispers. "You found one." His gaze shifts back to me. "Minnow, I..."

He leans in towards me. I barely have time to realise what is happening before it happens. Cillian softly presses his lips against mine. It is as if time is suspended – nothing else is happening, nothing else exists, just this moment as Cillian's lips caress my own.

He wraps his arms around my waist, one hand still holding the orange, and draws away from the kiss. There's a huge smile on his face.

I force a smile back, since I'm too overwhelmed to express my emotions properly in the moment. He kissed me. He kissed me. Cillian kissed me! This man, this handsome man full of charm and softness and courage could have chosen anyone in the world, and he chose me. He's still holding me. Again, he makes me feel seen. I'm not just the baker's daughter. I'm someone special.

"I've tried to stop myself from doing that," admits Cillian. "But this time, I had to give in."

"I'm glad you did," I respond.

He puts the Blessed orange in his bag and gives it a quick pat. "Two things left, then. Hair from a black goat, and three stones from Haunted Lake."

My brow crinkles as I try to think. "I've never seen a black goat in Schlafhold."

"I've never even heard of one."

I say, "I know someone who might have."

CHAPTER 13

If Wave is as exhausted as we are when we arrive at the Schlafhold stables three days later, she hides it well. She plods along as always, her thick eyelashes blinking slowly. She hasn't had much to carry on the way back. Just a few leftover empty sacks and water-skins.

Haystack is out the front of the stables, emptying dirty water onto the ground. He looks up and smiles as we approach.

"If it isn't my favourite young woman!" he declares as he meets us. He takes Wave's reins, and then turns his attention to me. "And I suppose it's nice to see you too, Minnow."

I drop my mouth open in exaggerated indignation. He winks.

"Thank you for lending us Wave," says Cillian. "She performed her duties well."

"I wouldn't have offered her if she couldn't." Haystack smiles, but it is a stiff smile. "I imagine you both had a lovely time together?"

"Ha," I laugh. "If only. But we were hoping you could help us with something."

"Anything," insists Haystack.

"We're looking for a black goat. But we haven't the faintest idea where to find one."

Haystack frowns. "What do you want a goat for? You can hardly tame them. No use to farmers or as pets."

"We don't need to keep it," I try to explain. "Just get close enough to…" I don't know how to continue without giving too much away. I look to Cillian pleadingly.

"My aunt collects oddities," Cillian pipes up. "She's got a set of different-coloured goat hairs, but she's missing black. I thought you might be able to help."

Haystack thinks for a moment. "A horse-hair wouldn't do? I've got a couple of black horses."

"Has to be a goat."

"Well, there are a few wild goat herds in the hills to the east, north of Haunted Lake. I've been climbing out there and seen goats before, but I can't recall seeing a black one. But if there is a black goat anywhere near Schlafhold, that's where it'll be."

Cillian and I exchange glances.

Haystack continues, "I could take you there, if you like."

"I don't think-…" begins Cillian.

"That would be great," I say at the same time.

Haystack nods. "Those hills can be treacherous if you don't know the right places to step. I'll do my best to help. Won't make any promises about that goat, though."

I try to figure out when would be a good day for me to go. I've lost track of what day it is now! I have to be at the bakery every day except Saturday…

But then I remember Dad's words. *Don't feel you need to come back at all*. Well, if that's how he feels about me, why should I go to work on days I don't want to?

"Are we all free tomorrow?" I propose.

"Tomorrow?" Haystack rubs the back of his head. "Tomorrow's the Twilight Festival, ain't it?"

The Twilight Festival. I'd forgotten all about it. Schlafhold's yearly celebration of the upcoming end of winter. It's a local affair, but a special one.

"What Twilight Festival?" asks Cillian.

"It's a celebration we have," explains Haystack. "There'll be music, Poppy's famous vegetable stew, cakes... There will be cakes, won't there, Minnow?"

My jaw drops. Dad and I always bake the cakes for the festival. Did he do it all himself while I was away?

"I... I think so," I say. "I guess we'll find out tomorrow. Do you think we could make it to the hills and back before dark?"

Haystack sticks out his bottom lip and nods. "As long as we keep up a good pace, sure."

"Great," I say. Then, "Does anyone mind if I invite Thivya along?" I know she probably won't be able to come, but I don't want her to feel left out.

Haystack shrugs. "Fine by me."

Cillian does too, but for some reason it looks like the spark in his eyes is missing.

"I'm back." I mean to call it out, but instead the words come out so softly that they wouldn't be heard across the other side of the room. The bakery is empty, anyway: it's just past sunset. Dad is nowhere to be seen. I notice a row of cakes lined up on a bench at the back of the store, iced with fruit on top. It must have taken Dad hours to prepare those.

I make my way out the back and into the cottage. There is a warm orange glow emanating from the window. I open the door and step inside.

Ma is seated in front of the fireplace, as she often is during the evenings when Dad is cooking. I can smell the earthy aroma of roasted potatoes.

I close the door behind me and drop my bag by the door. I kneel down to take out my purse.

"Did you find something?" Dad's voice startles me.

There it is again, that feeling of guilt. But I haven't done anything wrong.

He is standing with his arms crossed, his head tilted to the side slightly in a confrontational manner. Nevertheless, there is an inkling of hope in his tone of voice.

A hope I'm about to extinguish.

I shake my head, avoiding his gaze. "I've only got this." I place my purse on the table.

He hesitates and then opens it. He pokes around at the coins and nods approvingly. Then, "But nothing from... the man you went to see."

"I tried," I say.

He looks away.

"The cakes look good," I comment.

Dad says nothing.

"I'm sorry I forgot about the festival. Why didn't you remind me?"

"Would it have changed your mind?"

He's right. It wouldn't have made me stay.

"If you need help..." I begin.

"It's all done," says Dad stoutly. He brushes his hands on his apron. "There's a plate for you over there. Best to eat before it gets cold." Before I can thank him, he walks off.

I turn to Ma. She stares into the fire and I wonder, as always, if she observes each flicker of orange. Maybe they, awake and lively, are observing her.

My breath comes out in foggy spirals as I wake to another winter morning. Dad has already started in the bakery. I start getting ready to join him, but then remember that I won't be working today.

When I step outside, Cillian is leaning against the wall.

"You made me jump!" I exclaim.

"Apologies."

"What are you doing here? It's barely morning. We won't leave for hours."

"I really wanted to see you," he says, leaning towards me. He plants a soft kiss on my lips, sending a wave of... something through my body. Then he says, "And warn you."

"Warn me?"

"Yes. My cousin, Raina, has just arrived in town."

"Why does that warrant a warning?"

"Most of the time she doesn't cause trouble. But she can be a bit domineering. Fierce, maybe."

"You said I was fierce," I remind him.

Cillian hesitates. "It's different. Raina... likes to be the boss. And if she's not, she'll heckle from the sidelines."

I sigh. "Will she want to travel with us today?"

"Definitely. But I'll keep her in line."

"I can hold my own." I pout.

Cillian traces a finger along the side of my face. "You sure can." His finger stops at my chin. Out of nowhere, I start aching for him to keep moving his finger further, stroking my jawbone, caressing my neck. Oh, imagine what his lips would feel like on my neck. I might just lift off the ground.

"Raina knows about the Curse," Cillian explains. "But she's not coming because she wants to help. She just wants to stick her nose into my life."

"She sounds horrid."

Cillian laughs warmly. "She's not so bad once you know her, really. Just... keep your wits about you when she's around."

He turns to leave, but I grab his hand. He looks at me questioningly. I lean in and kiss him. We kiss slowly at first, sharing the warmth between our lips. He steps in even closer to me, so that our chests are pressed together. I have to tilt my head back.

Cillian steps away suddenly.

"What's wrong?" I ask.

He shakes his head. "If I don't go now... I'll never stop kissing you."

"That's a bit of a cliché," I chuckle.

The corner of his mouth curls in a smile. "Fine, then. If I don't go now, I won't be able to stop myself from doing a lot more than kissing you."

"Like what?" I probe, my heart hammering. What else is Cillian willing to do with me?

"Minnow..."

"Fine, fine, go and leave me here alone."

He rolls his eyes. "I'll see you in a couple of hours."

Thivya waits by the bridge with me, chattering away about how excited she is to have a day away from her siblings. She has packed a satchel full of snacks for us to share.

Haystack soon arrives and Thivya flings her arms around him.

"I haven't seen you in **days,**" she says. Then, less exuberantly, "**And** Helix... you know."

Haystack presses his lips together grimly. "Yeah. Pity, that."

"How is he?" I ask.

Haystack tilts his head to the side. "He's moving and talking, but he's real shaken up about the whole thing."

"Anyone would be," says Thivya.

"That leg of his isn't getting better, either," discloses Haystack. "Heron offered to chop it off, but he's just gonna keep it wrapped up. Heya, that must be Cillian's cousin." He nods back in the direction of the village.

Cillian is striding towards us alongside a thin, pale-skinned woman. She has luscious wavy black hair that reaches her shoulders, curling up at the ends. Something about her face says that she smiles a lot. A mischievous smile. There's a spring to her step as she walks beside Cillian, her skittery movements a noticeable contrast to his smooth, even steps. She is clearly in the middle of telling him some kind of narrative. When they reach us, she stops and looks up. She silently appraises each of us. Her gaze falls on me last. She's beautiful.

Her deep brown eyes are like libraries: just from looking at them, I can tell she is full of knowledge and wisdom. And whispers and dark corners.

She places her hands on her hips.

"Aren't you going to introduce yourself?" Cillian prompts.

"They all know who I am," shrugs Raina.

She's right. I already told Haystack and Thivya she would be joining us. I can see she's got a protection knife at her belt, but she doesn't take it out. Maybe customs are different where she comes from. Or maybe she just doesn't care if she comes across as rude.

Cillian sighs. "Alright, then. Haystack, lead the way."

The eastern hills are bathed in sunshine. Other than an occasionally nippy wind, it is a perfect day for adventuring.

It's almost midday when we reach the base of the hills. They are steeper than I expected, with rocks jutting out here and there.

"Where are the goats?" asks Thivya.

"They roam all around," explains Haystack. "But they prefer it up high."

After a bite to eat, we begin the ascent. I feel the strain on my knees pretty quickly. I think I'll have sore calf muscles tomorrow, too.

Raina walks at the back. Maybe I'm imagining it, but I can feel her gaze on me, like a prickle between my shoulder blades. What is she thinking about me?

"There's a good lookout here," says Haystack, ushering us over to a rocky outcrop. Facing northeast, we peer into the distance.

"There!" exclaims Thivya. "I can see something moving!"

I look in the direction she is pointing. Sure enough, there are moving shapes near the base of another hill.

"Aye, those'll be the goats," says Haystack.

"How will we get close enough without scaring them away?" I ask.

"Depends how much they've been around people," replies Haystack. "They might pay us no notice. Or they might bolt as soon as they hear our footsteps. Only one way to find out."

"What's that?" Raina asks, but she isn't looking in the same direction as the rest of us.

We turn simultaneously. Raina nods towards the south, where a conglomeration of ruins lie. Beyond them is a wide, dark lake.

"Haunted Lake," whispers Cillian. "It's closer than I thought."

"No-one ought to ever go there again," Haystack mutters.

Cillian turns back to face the direction of the goats, but I can tell the lake is still on his mind.

We make our way down the hill. As we approach the goats, a few of them pause their munching and look up at us with piercing stares.

The goats are all different colours – white, chestnut, apricot, maroon, and patchworks of many. Finally, I see it – an all-black male goat tugging at some weeds wedged between two rocks.

"You know, it's probably easier if we just kill it," says Raina casually. "Otherwise, we could be chasing it all day."

Thivya crinkles up her nose. "I am *not* killing a goat."

"No-one said *you* have to do it," responds Raina, taking out a slingshot from her pocket. She kneels down and flips a few stones over in her hands, weighing them up. She clearly knows what she is doing.

Haystack looks horrified. "No, I'm sure that's not necessary at all. We ought to at least try and approach it first."

Raina shrugs. "Go ahead. But I'll be ready if it bolts."

Haystack shoots Cillian a dark glare which clearly means *I can't believe you brought your evil cousin along.*

As we grow nearer, the closest goats begin to turn and wander away. The rest will doubtlessly follow suit. We are going to need a new plan, and hopefully not one that involves a slingshot.

"Maybe just one of us should go," suggests Haystack. "Then we'd appear less threatening."

"Who, then?" asks Thivya.

"Haystack, you're good with animals," I point out.

"I know horses," Haystack replies. "Not goats."

"Same thing," sighs Raina. "Come on, if we don't get this over and done with soon, it'll be dark when we get back."

Before I can stop myself, I turn to her and snap, "Why did you even come if you don't want to be here?"

Raina raises her eyebrows, taken aback. "Whoa. Okay. Didn't realise you got ticked off so easily."

Cillian elbows her. "Drop it, Raina."

"Raina does kind of have a point, though," Thivya says. "It's getting late, and it'll be freezing once the sun sets. And I want to be back in time for the festival."

Everyone is silent for a moment.

I look to Cillian. Surely he wants to try and get the goat hair, given he's the one who needs it for the Counterspell?

Cillian doesn't say anything.

Well, someone has got to do it. "I'll go," I announce.

Without waiting for a response, I continue towards the herd of goats. I feel their eyes boring into me, but none of them move. Some continue eating, while others stiffen and face me apprehensively.

I am close now. I fix my attention on the black one as I pass the other goats, careful not to make any loud noises. They shy away but don't bolt.

I slow down even more as I draw closer to the black goat. It is still gnawing on the weeds in the rocks, either oblivious or indifferent to my presence. A few more steps, and I can reach out my hand...

"Minnow!" I hear a cry on the wind, and it doesn't sound like someone cheering me on.

I glance back over my shoulder to where the others are standing. Thivya has a hand over her mouth. Haystack's mouth has dropped open. Raina grips her slingshot by her side.

Cillian is pointing at something. "Minnow, look out! Don't move!"

I look to where Cillian is pointing: upwards and to my right. There is a hillside with a rocky outcrop, with one large rock in particular jutting out sideways so that it hangs over the hill slightly.

I feel a sense of dread in my stomach, even before I see it. There, perched on the rock, is a huge creature with the head of an eagle. Its beady eyes are fixed on me. It is not an eagle, however. Its front two legs are talons, but its body and hind legs are those of a lion. Tucked at its sides are massive wings.

A griffin.

I've seen them fly in small groups over the village a couple of times, but they have always been so far up that they are barely distinguishable from birds. This is definitely bigger than a bird. It's bigger than me. I guess it is on the hunt for lunch, and I've ended up amongst its prey.

The griffin cocks its head to the side slightly. Its beak quivers a little. What is it thinking?

I try to remember everything I know about griffins, but it's hard to latch onto a single thought when I'm being scrutinised by the intimidating creature. They are supposed to live a long way away, for starters. High in the mountains. They steal livestock. They hoard treasures in big nests. They can very easily scoop up a human and eat them for dinner.

My heart begins hammering in my chest until my own heartbeat is all I can hear. I feel the blood pumping in my ears and temples.

As I watch the griffin, it rises onto its legs. A shiver passes through its body, causing a feather to drop loose.

I glance back to my friends.

"Come back, Minnow!" calls Haystack.

"No, don't move!" instructs Cillian. "It'll attack faster if it thinks you're trying to run away."

He draws his knife and begins making his way towards me.

I turn my attention briefly back to the black goat. It's only a few paces away. I take half a step closer. It doesn't react. I take another step and reach out my hand.

An overwhelming, billowing wind emanates from above, tousling my hair uncomfortably and sending a cold shiver down my body. Without looking up, I know that the griffin has taken flight.

It hasn't descended straight down, though. The griffin soars through the air towards where the others stand, its talons curled underneath its furry body. Its wide wings beat loudly like drum hits through the air. I can almost feel them.

It is high in the air when it reaches the others, but they all duck to the ground anyway. The griffin isn't interested in them, however. It swerves sharply and circles back in my direction. Those sharp black eyes are fixed on me. The talons begin to uncurl. Its beak opens and it lets out a harsh cry: a squawk with the guttural ferocity of a roar.

CHAPTER 14

I watch as a stone collides with the griffin's backside. The griffin continues its trajectory, oblivious or at least undeterred. Raina loads another stone into her slingshot.

I'm ready to give in to my impending doom, when I see Cillian running towards me. My heart skips at the sight of him. Those tangled curls, those caring hazel eyes. It pains me that I won't get to hold him a final time. Feel his warm embrace.

The griffin is seconds away.

I can't die here. Not so far from home, not in front of my friends. Not without saying goodbye to Cillian.

I reach for my protection knife, but realise it will be of no use against such a monstrous creature with the upper hand. I look around for anything that might help me fight, or help me hide...

The only thing next to me is the black goat. The goat lets out a frenzied, grating scream as it sees the griffin approaching.

I lunge towards the goat and grab it by its horns. It tugs away, but I keep my grip firm. I pull it forwards until it is positioned between me and the oncoming griffin. Then, I duck down, using it as cover...

The goat is ripped away. A distressed bleat erupts and fades as the goat is swiftly carried away by the griffin.

Cillian reaches me, breathless. "Minnow, quick! In case it comes back!" He reaches a hand out to me.

"Wait," I say. I bend down and retrieve a single black goat hair from the ground. I hold it up to Cillian.

He beams. "You did it."

Haystack stumbles towards us. "Bless you, Minnow, you're okay," he says, placing a hand on his heart.

I nod, and realise I'm shaking. "Let's go."

As we get back to Schlafhold, the sound of music emanating from plucked strings reaches our ears. The Twilight Festival has begun. Normally the dulcet tones of Helix's flute would be mingled among the lutes and harps, but not this year.

Lanterns have been strung up along the main street, creating a yellowish haze. A huge table stands in the middle of the street. Every inch of it is covered in food: platters of fruit, Dad's cakes, roast meats, goblets of wine, and a big metal pot filled to the brim with chunky vegetable stew. A bonfire blazes nearby.

Thivya breathes in deeply. "I don't know if I've ever felt this hungry in my life. Being scared out of your wits makes you hungry, apparently. Boy, that stew looks good."

Thivya drifts towards the table.

I glance around, trying to spot Dad. He's not at the table, and he's not among the revellers dancing by the musicians. He doesn't seem to be among any of the villagers chatting by the bonfire, either.

"Would you like something to eat, Minnow?" asks Cillian.

I would, but not yet. I reek. My body odour wafts into my nostrils, and I'm sure it will reach everyone else's soon enough. All the sweat from climbing – and being terrified – has seeped into my clothing. The last thing I want to do is hang around Cillian like a bad smell – literally.

"I'll meet you back out here soon," I say. "Just give me a few minutes." Before Cillian can ask any questions, I hurry towards home.

"Where have you been?" Dad's voice is a grumble. He sits with Ma by the fire, running a brush through her hair.

"Out with my friends," I declare nonchalantly.

Dad raises an eyebrow. "You've given up on the bakery, then?"

"Just taking some time off."

"Given up on your Ma, too?"

Guilt begins to churn in my stomach. "No."

"Well, I've looked after her today. As you can see. So you might as well go enjoy the festivities." His voice is weighed down with resentment.

I want to tell him about the griffin, but I know it will just make him angry to hear about me being in danger.

"Are you going to come out and celebrate?" I ask. "The stew smells delicious."

Dad puts down the brush and sighs. "No. I'm where I want to be." He places a gentle hand on Ma's back and tries to catch her eye. She doesn't look his way.

After I've washed and changed into a fresh set of clothes, I re-emerge onto the street. The air is buzzing with excitement. The music has picked up into a lively jig.

I find Cillian outside Mr Gust's miscellaneous goods shop. Mr Gust's wares are on display out the front of the shop in an attempt to snare a few extra customers. Everything from wind chimes to teapots to buttons are arrayed on a table. Cillian is rifling through a pile of old books.

"You like reading?" I ask, sidling up to him.

"I just wanted to see if there was anything on, you know…" his voice drops to a whisper. "Haunted Lake. But I haven't had any luck."

Mr Gust approaches us, drumming his long spindly fingers together. "Can I interest you in some paints? We have blue, red, green…"

"I'm not much of an artist," I admit.

"We're making a mural," explains Mr Gust, "To commemorate the festival." He points to the wall at the side of the shop. It is adorned with freshly-painted images: leaves, snowflakes, hand prints and swathes of colours blending into each other.

"It's beautiful," I say, taking a step closer.

"Why the snowflakes?" asks Cillian. "It's not snowing."

"It's because the Twilight Festival celebrates the transition of winter into spring," I say. "We treasure the last breath of winter while welcoming the oncoming spring. That's why it's called the Twilight Festival – it's like the twilight, an in-between time. So, the snowflakes symbolise the winter."

"Please, take some paints and add your own touches," insists Mr Gust.

"I fear my contribution would be but a blemish," says Cillian. "Art is not my strength either."

"Then, please, do a hand print," says Mr Gust, holding out a platter smeared in purple paint.

We give in, and Cillian and I each press a hand into the paint. We choose a spot near the bottom of the wall, underneath a pattern of leaves. I place my left hand on the wall, leaving a print. Cillian uses his right hand, and leaves a print next to mine so that our thumbs are touching. It brings me joy: from now on whenever I pass this wall, I will remember the first winter Cillian and I spent together.

We wash the paint off our hands as the music changes to a slower tune. Cillian extends a hand to me.

"Will you dance with me, Minnow?"

I hesitate. While I occasionally dance on my own, I never have in front of an audience.

"No-one will be looking," says Cillian, as if reading the worry written on my face.

I tentatively take his hand. He draws me in close. I breathe in that forest smell, and it relaxes my body. This is where I'm meant to be.

He reaches down and places a hand on the small of my back. We move in time with the music, not going far, just rocking back and forth with the melody.

"Tell me something about you I don't know," says Cillian, gazing into my eyes.

"Hmm," I reply. "The first time I left Schlafhold and went to Harethorn, I was so scared that I never left my Dad's side. I pretty much clung onto his arm like stickyweed."

"How old were you?"

"Eight, maybe? Old enough that I should have been braver. Your turn. Tell me something I don't know about you."

"I'll do a childhood story, too. When I was about five, my sister pushed me into a pond and I got bitten on the hand by a fish."

"By a fish?!"

Cillian chuckles. "It didn't leave a mark. But for ages I was wary of fish at the markets, worried that they would spring back to life and nip me."

I laugh.

"He was always a sensitive child," Raina sighs. How long has she been standing there watching us with her hands on her hips?

Of course she wants to disrupt our time together. Cillian was right about her being a menace.

Cillian lets go of me and turns to Raina. "Since you're so keen to be part of the conversation, why don't you tell us something we don't know about you?"

Raina looks at him through narrowed eyes. "You know plenty about me."

"Minnow doesn't."

Raina crosses her arms. "Fine. When I was... younger... I used to spar for money. People would place bets and I would fight other contestants in an arena while the gamblers watched."

"Did you win?" I ask.

Raina scoffs. "Obviously. Made lots of money, too. People didn't often bet on a scrawny teenage girl. But I was taught to fight at school. It's normal where I come from."

Cillian clears his throat. "How about something to eat?"

Raina tags along as we go to the feasting table. Poppy's vegetable stew has almost run out, so Cillian and I share a bowl while Raina digs into a bag of roasted chestnuts.

The cold starts to gnaw at me, and the villagers begin to disperse as the night grows darker. When it is time to go, Cillian pulls me aside, out of Raina's earshot.

"Meet me tomorrow morning on the edge of the forest," he whispers.

CHAPTER 15

The ground is dry in the morning – it wasn't cold enough to frost over overnight. I reach the first line of oak trees and take a look around.

Cillian steps out from behind a trunk. "Minnow." He opens his arms wide, inviting me in. I step forwards and let him embrace me. He rubs his hand down my spine.

"Do you still want to go to Haunted Lake?" I ask.

"Eventually, yes," says Cillian. "But that's not why I wanted to meet you."

"Oh?" I frown.

"I just wanted to see you," he admits, bringing his hand to my forehead and tucking my hair behind my ear.

I tilt my head back and look up at him. "Well, you've seen me."

"Maybe I wanted to do more than see you. Maybe I wanted to kiss you."

He leans in and brushes his lips against mine, just for a moment. It's a minuscule movement, but it makes my heart flutter.

"You could have died yesterday," Cillian whispers. "I was terrified."

"But I didn't."

"You didn't. And you got the goat's hair. I have to thank you for that." He plants a kiss on my forehead and gives me a squeeze. "You're so soft."

He begins kissing me on the lips again, more passionately this time. I let his strength guide me backwards until my back is pressed against a flat tree trunk. One of Cillian's hands runs over my abdomen and around the curve of my back. The other draws a line over my collarbone. I wrap my arms around him. He's so close to me. Then, he moves both hands so they cover my breasts. I breathe in sharply. He begins massaging them softly. My nipples harden. At the same time, I feel a tingle between my legs.

"Cillian," I whisper into his lips.

"Mm?"

"I'm just saying your name. Cillian."

I feel his smile press against me. He takes my left nipple between his forefinger and thumb and rolls it around slightly. Somehow, it produces a feeling like an itch down below, where a slickness is developing between my thighs.

I take his hand and guide it down towards my crotch, lifting the waistband of my skirt and underwear so he can reach underneath.

"Are you sure this is what you want?" he checks.

"Yes."

A moment later, his finger starts tracing the shape of my vulva, following a line between my lips before resting on the tip of my clit. He slowly starts circling my clit. Each movement sends a shudder through my body. I let out a small gasp.

"That feel good?"

I nod, unable to speak for the moment.

He continues toying with my clit, and it feels like there is a pressure building up inside me. A mountain of pleasure with a looming avalanche. I moan.

The circling and sliding feels good – feels heavenly – but it's not enough.

"More..." I moan.

"More than this?"

My lower body clenches and I know exactly what I want.

"I want you inside of me."

"Mm..." he hums, and the sound turns me on so much that I feel an ache.

Now that I've said it, I realise how desperate I am.

As his finger leaves my clit and traces downwards, I twist with the agony of missing him.

But then I feel his finger slipping smoothly inside me. I hadn't realised just how wet I am.

I'm overwhelmed by the thought: *Cillian Gray is inside of me. He's the closest he's ever been to me.*

Unable to restrain myself, I push myself down and around his delving digit. My muscles clench around him, and he lets out a gasp. I place my hand over his trousers and feel a hard bulge. A large hard bulge.

My heart skips a beat. I cradle the shape of him, applying a tiny bit of pressure. Cillian groans. The sound makes me tighten around him again.

I withdraw my hand and then slide it under his trousers, so I am touching his skin directly. I've never felt a penis before. I wrap my fingers around it, and I am surprised by the way his skin moves.

He gasps. "Yes... touch me... just like that."

I trace my hand along the length of his shaft, pausing at the tip. I imagine the tip penetrating inside of me, what it would feel like to be connected to Cillian that way. I flush with heat.

He holds his finger still inside me. Then, he slowly begins moving it in and out, but never fully coming out. Good thing, too, because I can't cope with the idea of him coming out. I want him inside me forever.

I lace my fingers around his cock again. "Tell me what feels good for you." I start stroking.

"That... that feels good," he manages. He looks me in the eyes. "You really are the most beautiful thing I have ever seen."

Suddenly it doesn't feel like enough. I want more of him. All of him. I increase the speed with which I'm stroking him, and I use my other hand to dig my nails into his back. He gets the message and slips another finger inside of me. It's a tight fit at first, but it makes me feel wonderfully full. Full of Cillian Gray.

I buck my hips and grind into him, willing him to be deeper and faster.

Cillian lets out a breathy grunt. "You have to slow down... Or else I'm going to come."

"And you don't want that?"

Cillian hesitates. "I just want to be yours. And I want you to be mine."

I nod. "I want that too."

He kisses me on the lips.

His lips still on mine, he speeds up the pace with which he is moving in and out of me. I can barely focus on each movement. Everything is happening at once. Every breath I take is short and sharp. I keep stroking his dick. He pulls away from the kiss: his head is tilting back as his face scrunches in bliss. Moments later, I feel a sticky wetness in his pants. I pause the stroking.

"Minnow... Minnow..." he whispers my name as if it were a prayer.

I clench around his fingers and my whole body goes tight. Then, he slips his fingers out of my vagina and starts quickly stroking my clit. It only takes a couple of seconds for me to come. Warmth and pleasure dance through every inch of my body. I'm breathless. I worry for a second that I might need to stop and do my breathing exercises, but thankfully it becomes easier to breathe as my heartbeat slows.

Cillian withdraws his hand. He is similarly exhausted.

"I'm going to sit down," I say, sliding down the tree trunk.

Cillian sits beside me. I rest my head on his shoulder and wrap my arm around his front.

We sit here for a while, just breathing.

"So," I say at last. "Haunted Lake."

Cillian presses his lips together.

I continue, "I imagine you want to get it over and done with as soon as possible, now that you've got the other items?"

"Minnow, I've been thinking... I don't think you should come with me."

I frown. "Why not?" There's an indignant lilt in my voice.

Cillian shakes his head. "It's too dangerous. If there is actually a Twisted there – or multiple Twisteds – it'll be unsafe."

"Everywhere else has been unsafe."

"Exactly. I've seen you almost come to harm too many times. I would never forgive myself if something happened to you."

"But what about you?" I counter. "You're in far more danger if you go alone."

Cillian sighs.

"I have an idea," I say. "Let's scout it first. Just go to the edge of the ruins and get a sense of what's there. Then we can make a proper plan."

Cillian's face wrinkles as he considers this.

"We'll just take a look," I insist. "We can come back for the stones once we know what we're up against."

After a moment, Cillian nods. "Okay."

I change into a pair of cream-coloured trousers and pull on a tough brown jacket. I sheathe my protection knife at my belt. I tie my hair back into a loose ponytail.

I step out into the street to meet Cillian and feel a bubble of disappointment in my gut as I see that Raina is waiting alongside him. I had hoped it would just be Cillian and I, alone with each other...

Raina smirks at me as I approach. Cillian smiles as warmly as ever.

We start to walk towards the bridge. I go to position myself next to Cillian, but Raina quickly slots herself beside him, so she's standing between us.

"You know the history of Haunted Lake, I'm guessing," says Raina.

"No, actually," I admit.

Raina makes a clicking sound with her tongue. Disapproving? Mocking? She continues, "I studied history at the Broadfinch Academy."

Good for you, I want to say. I don't know why she irks me so much. Then I remember her firing her slingshot at the griffin yesterday, and decide to cut her some slack.

"You went to the Academy?" I ask.

"Yes. A few years ago now."

The Broadfinch Academy is the only post-school educational institution outside of the Amber City. The only Schlafhold citizen I know of who went to the Academy is Heron, who studied medicine there.

"People lived by Haunted Lake over a thousand years ago. It was a fishing village, of course, and also home to several great philosophers. A thriving community. They traded regularly with the surrounding towns, including Schlafhold. But this was a long time ago, obviously."

"What happened?" I ask.

"They disappeared," replies Raina.

"Where to?"

"Nowhere." Raina shrugs. "One day, a trading party arrived and found the village completely deserted. Not a soul remained."

"My friends saw a Twisted there," I tell her. "Maybe the village was attacked."

"There would have been signs of a fight," Raina counters. "Gnawed bones at the least. But there was nothing."

"Maybe they fled to a nearby village?"

Raina shrugs again. "There's no record of it. No big population changes recorded anywhere." She pauses. Then, "It's said that when you walk through the remains of the village, you hear the voices of its citizens wailing. That's how it earned the name 'Haunted Lake'."

Goosebumps tickle my arms.

We're about halfway there, when someone appears on the path ahead. I soon recognise it as Sal. She beams at us with her toothy grin.

"Good morning Minnow, Cillian and... Raina?" she raises an eyebrow as she recognises Cillian's cousin.

"Long time, no see," responds Raina in a sing-song voice.

Sal's smile fades slightly. "Where are you all off to?"

"Haunted Lake," replies Raina before I can jump in with a less truthful answer.

Sal stares at Raina for a moment, and then turns to me. "I don't know if that's a good idea. After what happened to poor Helix..."

"We can take care of ourselves," Raina insists. "What are you doing out here, anyway?"

"I was just taking some cheese to the Lowry farm. Mister Lowry has been ill. You three be careful, okay?"

I nod. Raina rolls her eyes.

"I assure you, we plan to leave at the first sign of any trouble," says Cillian.

Sal looks wary, but says no more and continues on her way.

I glance over at Raina. "It sounds like you have a history with Sal."

Raina waves a hand dismissively. "I've met her a few times. We shared a meal last time I visited Schlafhold."

"I didn't know you'd been to Schlafhold before," I say. I've certainly never seen her. I would remember a face like hers.

"Only briefly," sighs Raina. "I drop in to see Betty every now and again. But I don't stay for long. Can't stand the smell of all the mud and animals."

"Typical city girl," I mutter.

Raina mutters something in return. I barely make out the phrase "country bumpkin".

I'm about to come up with another retort, but then I see it in the distance: a smattering of stone ruins and a wide, black mass of water.

Haunted Lake.

CHAPTER 16

Cillian, Raina and I approach the outskirts of the ruined village. Most buildings are battered husks of what they used to be, half-crumbled stone and wood structures worn down by time and weather. The majority of the buildings are perched on the edge of the lake, wrapping around a quarter of its perimeter. A few rotting wooden piers stretch out beyond the shoreline.

There's a bitter taste on the air. Metallic and salty.

The silence is eerie. The sound of our footsteps is an intrusion on a place which aches to be forgotten.

My hand drifts towards the hilt of my protection knife. If there is a Twisted here, it will hear us for sure.

Cillian pauses and glances around at our surroundings. "It seems safe enough. For now, at least. Maybe we have time to..." He beelines for the water. Raina and I follow.

I crinkle my nose as we get close to the water's edge. It's... disgusting. The water is murky and almost black, obscuring any sign of the bottom of the lake.

"We need a stick," decides Cillian. "An oar or something. To test the depth."

We glance around. I spot a stick and offer it to Cillian, but it's only just longer than my arm and doesn't appear to come close to reaching the bottom.

"I'll take a look in those ruins over there," says Raina, pointing a thumb towards the houses on the north side of the lake.

"Don't you think we should stick together?" I say.

"We can cover more ground if we spread out," responds Raina with a shrug.

I look to Cillian. He stares pensively at the water. He sure does like to stare at that lake. It does have a hypnotic quality.

"Cillian?" I prompt.

"I agree with Raina," he says quietly. "Just shout if you're in trouble. We won't be far."

I hesitate. I don't think it's a good idea. But I don't want to appear weak in front of either of them.

I make my way towards an old building. I draw my protection knife, gripping the hilt so hard that my hand hurts.

The building appears to be a hovel that has collapsed in on itself, although the front door remains standing. I notice a strange symbol carved into rock above the door frame: a spiral inside a square. I step through the doorway and evaluate the remains of the hovel. Splinters of wood and piles of rubble adorn the ground. I pick up a couple of pieces of wood, but they are mostly short, thick slabs.

There is a pile of objects in one corner of the roofless room. I kneel down and rummage through it. A couple of old fish bones, some broken ceramic shards, an empty glass bottle, a coil of old but solid rope. I guess anything of worth here would have been looted a long time ago. Wait, what's that?

I pick up a small wooden carving and examine it. It's a little bear. It reminds me of the wooden horse Haystack lent me. I have to remember to give that back to him.

I give up on this building, deciding there is nothing of use within. The building next door is much larger, and I figure it must be a place where people gathered. A town hall, perhaps? Again, I note a symbol atop the doorway: the same square with a spiral inside. What does it mean?

The large building is more intact, although the roof has caved in in the far corner. Rows of wooden benches, some splintered, some toppled, all dusty, face the far end of the room. At the front facing them is a tall wooden chair with a high back. I submit to the urge to go and sit in it. I make my way past the rows of benches, wrinkling my nose at the musty smell of the old wood. There's something else, too... Something more disgusting, more disturbing, but I don't recognise it. A smell that seems to bristle against my skin.

I reach the chair and sit on it. It creaks a little beneath my weight. I imagine everyone who has explored these ruins has come and sat on the chair, surveying the empty room. The hole in the roof doesn't dispel the dark gloom all around.

As I stare at the ground between the chair and the first row of benches, something catches my eye. Lines in the dust: long, thick lines as if someone had taken a broom and swept a random swirling pattern across the floor.

I walk over to one of the lines and press my hand against the floor. Whatever cleared this path has been here recently, as there is hardly any dust remaining.

Down on the ground, I notice something else: a large square shape on the floor. Upon closer inspection, I realise it's a trapdoor. The spiral within a square is carved onto its surface.

There is no handle or latch visible. Clearly, it's not meant to be easy to access. I wonder what could be underneath. A place for storing supplies?

I can't see any sign of the trapdoor being disturbed recently. Perhaps it's been shut since before the village was abandoned.

I try to dig my fingers into the groove at the edge, but they won't fit. I glance about in search of something I can insert underneath to prop it up. I spot a sliver of wood hanging off one of the benches. I snap it off and jam it into the crevice between the trapdoor and the floor.

It fits. I slip the piece of wood under the edge of the door and try to push it up. It's heavy, and for a moment I think the wood will break. But then the door lifts. I quickly grab it and push it aside.

A horrid stench billows out from the space below. It's the same smell I couldn't identify earlier, now magnified one hundred times. A wave of nausea rattles my body.

Plumes of dust waft through the air. I squint into the blackness beneath the trapdoor.

"What on earth is that smell?" Raina's voice behind me makes me jump. She wanders over, waving a hand in front of her face to ward off the odour.

"Look what I found," I say. I feel around the inside of the trapdoor's opening until I feel the solid rungs of a ladder bolted down.

Raina pokes the trapdoor lid with her toe. "I've seen that spiral symbol everywhere. You're not seriously going down there, are you?"

I shrug. "Might as well. I'm curious." I hesitate, pondering whether Raina is the type of person who would close the lid over the top of me as a joke. "You should come, too. I dare you."

Raina frowns. "You don't need to dare me. I'm not scared. Here, I'll even go first."

She reaches down and grabs the top of the ladder. She slowly descends into the darkness.

"Ugh," she scoffs. "I can barely breathe this air."

I follow her down.

Suddenly, Raina shrieks.

"What? What is it?" I call urgently, struggling to see downwards in the dark. I strain to listen, and hear Raina panting heavily.

"Minnow, stop," she yelps. "The ladder is broken. I can't hold on."

I look down and realise Raina is hanging onto the last remaining rung of the ladder with one hand, the rest of her dangling in thin air. She flings her spare hand into the air to try and grasp the rung, but misses.

"How far to the bottom?" I ask.

"Can't tell," gasps Raina.

"Here, I'll lower my leg and you can grab onto it."

"And pull you down, too? I don't fancy you falling on top of me." She lets out another yelp. "I'm slipping!"

"Just hold on," is all I can muster. Not very helpful.

Raina screams and I know she has let go of the ladder. I hear a *thud* below – not too far, by the sound of it. Then... silence.

"Raina?" No response. "Raina?"

I quickly climb back up and look around for anything that could help. I recall the rope from next door and rush out to grab it.

Once I've retrieved it, I look around for Cillian. He's not standing by the lake. I call his name, but the word is quickly consumed by the heavy, still air. There's no sign of him. I consider looking, but decide that the Raina issue is more urgent.

I tie a series of knots in the rope and then attach it to one of the ladder rungs. I slowly climb down the rope, using the knots as footholds. It is more difficult than I expected, with the rope swinging back and forth with each step. My hands start to burn from gripping the coarse material. Just as I think the rope isn't going to be long enough after all, I feel solid ground beneath me.

I step onto the ground and give my eyes a moment to adjust to the dark. I slowly get the sense that I am in a large space, perhaps as big as the hall above. I take a tentative step and something squishes underneath my foot. I bend down and realise it's Raina's arm. I kneel down and examine her. She's motionless, lying slightly curled up.

"Raina?" I whisper. I don't know why I whisper. Maybe it's the sense that something is very, very wrong nearby. I don't know what it is, but this place doesn't feel safe.

I shake Raina's shoulder. "Raina."

She lets out a quiet groan. "Ow..."

I let out a sigh of relief. At least she's alive.

"I fell..." she moans.

"Yes, you fell," I respond. "Are you hurt?"

She sits up and puts a hand to the back of her head. "I think I hit my head. Everything looks blurry."

"Can you stand up? Here." I offer her my hand.

Slowly, she takes it and rises to her feet. "You rescued me."

I laugh. "I got some rope, that's all."

"Like a knight in shining armour. But far more beautiful." Her words are slightly slurred. She must have hit her head *hard*. Still, the endearment softens something in me.

"What's that?" Raina points past me at a shape in the darkness. Now that I look, there are lots of shapes in the darkness. Objects scattered around the floor.

The feeling of unease in me grows. "I think we should go."

"You were the one who wanted to see what was down here."

She's right. Part of me still wants to know. I step towards the closest shape, which is barely illuminated by the light from the trapdoor opening.

It's a pile of something. Wood? No, hang on a second.

I bend down to take a closer look. It's...

Bones.

I gasp. "That's a skeleton. A human skeleton." I realise what the smell is now: death.

"What?" says Raina. She takes a look for herself. "Yuck."

I look around the room, and my eyes have adjusted to the dark enough now to see that there are dozens more skeletons scattered around. Dozens visible from here. Who knows how many more are spread out in the dark corners I can't see?

"What happened here...?" asks Raina.

"I don't know," I reply. "But I think we've solved the mystery of Haunted Lake."

"We've solved *half* the mystery," says Raina. "We found where the people went. But we don't know why."

Raina peers up at the broken ladder. The bottom half of it lies in pieces on the ground nearby.

"They must have become trapped down here after the ladder broke. But why was the whole village here in the first place?"

"They must have been hiding from something," I suggest. "That spiral symbol. Any idea what it means?"

Raina shakes her head. "Nothing in the history books about it."

"The people who came looking for them would have heard them crying out below but not known where they were," I realise. "That's why they thought the place was haunted. They could hear the villagers begging to be rescued. It wasn't ghosts."

"That's... grim," muses Raina.

"What could be so dangerous that a whole population would hide underground from it?" I query.

"A big storm, maybe?" suggests Raina. "Maybe the lake flooded."

"Would you go underground in a flood?"

"Good point. You don't think… you don't think there's still something out there, do you?"

"My friends saw a Twisted," I reply. "Or at least they think they did."

"A Twisted isn't that bad," says Raina. "Not everyone-hide-underground bad. They could have fought it off."

"We should leave Haunted Lake," I decide. "Let's get Cillian and go."

We pull ourselves up the rope and emerge back into the dusty hall. The silence feels even more eerie now that an extra threat lurks at the back of our minds.

"Huh, look at that," Raina says, going over to a fallen bench and picking up something I hadn't noticed before: a tattered old book with a worn brown cover.

"Let's get out of here," I insist, heading for the door.

"No, wait," responds Raina, holding up a hand as she reads a page of the book. "Listen to this: 'Mark the sign of the serpent to bar its entry'." She holds up the book, and I take a look at the open page. There's a large illustration of a snake, coiled in a spiral shape.

I look down at the trapdoor and the spiral painted on top. A serpent. Next, my gaze wanders to the lines in the dust. The lines are paths, the pattern of a slithering creature. But if that's the case, the creature must be *huge*. Its body must be almost as thick as my torso. And its length... impossible to tell.

"We need to get out. Now," I urge.

Raina still has her nose in the book. "I think it's safe to say that marking the sign of the serpent didn't help anyone." She snaps the book shut. "Just an old mythology tome. They must have been a superstitious bunch."

I shake my head. "It's real, Raina. Something was here. It still is." I point to the slither-marks on the floor.

"But there's no such thing..." Raina's voice trails away as she takes a look.

"Minnow! Raina!" Cillian's voice booms from outside.

Raina and I exchange a quick glance and then rush outdoors.

Cillian is standing just outside, his knife drawn. Alarmed, I follow his gaze to see... Not a serpent. Not at all.

Ambling towards us at great speed is a Twisted, teeth bared against black gums.

CHAPTER 17

It looks almost exactly as the stories described it. I had always imagined Twisteds to be twice as tall as me, but this one would only reach my nose when standing up straight. Everything else matches what I imagined: bark-like skin and loping long limbs, stretched vertical eyes with yellow-rimmed pupils, wolf teeth encased in a slightly protruding jaw. It makes a wheezing sound, a high-pitched whistling, as it staggers towards us. Almost like someone laughing so hard they can't breathe.

"What do we do?" I ask, knowing we only have moments left to act.

"You run," advises Cillian. "I'll hold it off."

Raina draws her slingshot and lets a stone fly loose in the direction of the Twisted. It clips the creature on the side of the head. It pauses momentarily, but then continues loping towards us.

"Go!" cries Cillian. "There's no time."

"Listen, Cillian," I say. "There is something else out here. We need to leave together."

But Cillian isn't listening. He's getting into a defensive position, knife raised. "Behind me! Now!"

I obey.

The Twisted pounces on Cillian, snapping at his wrist with its pointed teeth. Cillian lurches his arm out of the way and brings the hilt of his knife down on the Twisted's head. This only enrages the Twisted, which backs away and then squats down, preparing to spring forwards again.

I draw my knife. Cillian sees this out of the corner of his eye.

"No, Minnow! Run!"

"Cillian, please, you have to come too!"

"She's right," says Raina. "We all need to go."

The Twisted leaps into the air, this time aiming for Cillian's throat. It knocks him to the ground. The force of it causes him to drop his knife.

I charge forwards and stab wildly in the direction of the Twisted. I manage to miss it altogether.

Cillian holds the Twisted back with his bare hands while it gnashes its teeth in front of his face. Each chomp of the air gets closer to his nose.

I raise my arm, ready to strike again, but Raina grabs my elbow and pulls me back.

"What are you doing?!" I cry. Raina keeps tugging me along.

Raina shakes her head urgently and then points to the ground a dozen paces behind the Twisted.

Surging along the ground in Cillian's direction is a huge serpent. It is at least thirty feet long, and wide enough to swallow a person whole. Its scales are glossy black. An equally black tongue flicks out of its mouth.

My body turns cold and goosebumps tickle my skin. I'm struck by the perfect beauty of the serpent – so fluid in its movements, so smooth, unblemished despite being at least centuries old. Its eyes are a bottomless black, betraying no thought.

"Cillian," I call through gritted teeth, trying not to attract the serpent's attention.

Raina lets loose a stone from her slingshot and it whacks the Twisted in the eye. The Twisted pulls back, providing Raina with enough time to rush forwards and kick it in the side.

"Argh!" Raina cries out. The Twisted's skin was more solid than she expected.

Cillian wriggles away from the Twisted's grip and grabs his knife. He turns back to attack the Twisted again, but that's when he sees the serpent.

Cillian's eyes widen. He freezes, just as I have. At that moment, the serpent charges at him, thrusting its head forwards in a motion so fast I barely see it.

Cillian staggers backwards just in time. The serpent pulls its head back, but I can tell it is preparing to strike again.

"Run!" I cry out.

Cillian begins running towards me.

Meanwhile, Raina has grabbed a brick and is slamming it into the head of the Twisted. Dark blood splatters. The Twisted lets out a harsh cry like a strangled bird and then goes silent as Raina brings down the brick a final time. Raina lets out a satisfied sigh, but her relief is short-lived. She looks up and sees the serpent staring directly at her, its black eyes fixed on her crouched figure.

Raina turns on her heel and runs towards us. Suddenly, she stumbles and falls face-first.

I rush towards her. I'm vaguely aware that Cillian attempts to snatch at my shirt and stop me, but I've already leapt out of his reach.

The serpent slithers towards Raina. I reach her first and extend my hand to help her up.

"Thanks," she mutters. We turn together, ready to run, when I hear the *whoosh* of something zipping through the air towards me.

I look around just in time to see two enormous fangs flash through the air, ready to snap me up into a hungry pink mouth. The space between the fangs makes me briefly think of Cillian's missing tooth.

A blur passes in front of me. I squeeze my eyes shut. I hear a sharp gasp, and at first I think it's come from me. I wait for the pain.

But it doesn't come.

I open my eyes and see Raina in front of me, facing the serpent. She holds her arm above her face, as if shielding herself.

She stumbles backwards, bumping into me.

"Go, go!" she commands, spinning around and giving me a shove.

I do as she says and run away, reassured by the sound of her feet pattering on the ground behind me. Less reassured by the sound of the serpent sliding along behind her.

Sweat prickles my brow as we keep running. Cillian joins us. Finally, we reach the edge of the Haunted Lake village and climb a small hill. I dare a glance back over my shoulder. No sign of the serpent.

I feel my chest beginning to tighten, which is always bad news.

"I need to stop," I pant, holding up a hand.

The others slow down and look around.

"There it is," says Cillian, pointing to the bottom of the hill. The serpent has turned around and appears to be heading back into the ruins.

I take a few deep breaths, trying not to panic at the feeling of my throat constricting. Heron taught me long ago that panicking only makes it worse.

"Minnow, what's wrong?" Cillian's voice is laced with concern.

I wave my hand dismissively, not wanting to talk. I'll have to boil some water as soon as I get home. Heron might have some herbs I can burn as well. I think I can manage until then.

"Okay, I'm ready," I say after a couple of minutes, straightening up. I flash Cillian a warm smile.

He isn't smiley at all. "We'll never be able to get past that thing to retrieve the stones. It knows our scent now."

"I'm sure we can figure something out," I assure him.

"We'd have to kill it," says Cillian. "But we can't even get close without it striking us."

"So, we kill it from a distance," I say. "Raina's slingshot might not suffice, though."

I look to Raina. She is staring blankly into the distance and appears to be trembling slightly.

"Raina?" I prompt.

Raina holds out her arm. On her forearm are two round red blotches, each about the size of a fingerprint. Streaks of black under her skin are spreading from the wounds.

I realise what has happened. She got bitten. She jumped in front of me and took the bite.

"I don't feel well," murmurs Raina. She blinks slowly.

Cillian gasps. "You need to lie down. Slow the venom."

"No," I argue. "We need to get back to Schlafhold. Heron can heal her."

Cillian bites his lip. "Okay. Raina, come here. I'll carry you."

I can see Raina's face contort as she prepares to argue, but then she wobbles on the spot and appears to change her mind.

Cillian scoops her up. We begin the journey back to Schlafhold. Raina's eyelids flutter and then close.

CHAPTER 18

Cillian practically drops Raina onto the table in the centre of Heron's apothecary. Sweat trickles down the side of his temple.

Heron spots the wounded arm immediately and lifts it up. Her eyebrows arch as she queries, "Venom?"

Cillian and I nod.

Raina is unresponsive. Occasionally her eyes open halfway, but they soon close again.

"But what could possibly...?" Heron's voice trails away.

I tell her about the serpent at Haunted Lake. I think for a moment she is going to berate us for going out there, but she shakes her head quickly and turns her attention back to Raina.

"Out. I need to focus." She waves us away.

Cillian and I sit outside the apothecary, leaning against the dusty wall at the side of the building.

He runs his hands through his hair, an anxious habit. "Do you think Raina will be alright?"

"I know Heron will do everything she can to help her," I reach out and take his hand, rubbing my thumb gently over his. He looks down at this and squeezes my hand.

We sit in silence for a while, listening to footsteps and horse hooves pass by on the main road.

"I shouldn't have brought either of you with me," Cillian says.

"That's not true," I argue. "We might have never seen you again if you went alone."

He clenches his jaw. I realise he's trying not to cry.

"I don't want her to die because of me," Cillian whispers, his lip trembling.

"She won't die. And if she did, it wouldn't be because of you."

"Maybe not. Maybe you could blame the Curse. The damned Curse that follows me wherever I go. The Curse I will never be able to get rid of now."

"I have an idea," I tell him. "We can't get up close to that serpent. But we know someone who could attack it from afar. Abby, the archer from Yammoor we met in Walnut Woods."

Cillian considers this. His expression lightens somewhat. "You're right. We might still stand a chance." He gets up. "We'll find her first thing tomorrow morning. You'll come with me?"

I beam, glad to be invited this time.

He plants a kiss on my forehead and then heads in the direction of Betty's home.

It's not yet dark, so I am surprised to find the bakery empty and unattended. The sign on the door reads 'CLOSED UNTIL FURTHER NOTICE'. A prickle goes up my spine. Something is wrong.

I make my way into the cottage out the back. The living room is cold. I light the fire, letting a small flame spring to life.

"Minnow? Is that you?" Dad's voice echoes out from my parents' bedroom.

"It's me," I respond, following the direction of his voice.

I lean against the doorway of the bedroom, peering in.

Dad is stooped over the bed, holding a wet rag to Ma's forehead. "She's got a fever. Look how she's shivering."

"Have you spoken to Heron?"

Dad shakes his head. "It's only been a few hours. I came in to feed her at lunch and she was burning up."

In the half-light, I notice the bags underneath Dad's eyes. His face seems more gaunt and wrinkled than ever.

"Here, let me take over," I say, going over to join them.

"Stop," instructs Dad, holding up a hand.

I stop, confused.

He continues, "Were you at Haunted Lake today?"

I say nothing.

"Sal saw you near the Lowry farm. She was real worried for you."

I look down. There is no point denying it.

Dad continues, "The one place I told you not to go. It's not safe there. There's something... evil."

I frown. "You knew... You knew about the serpent!"

Dad narrows his eyes. "Serpent? Yes, that makes sense. We found something there when I was young... a crinkled, papery material. Like a snakeskin, but... giant."

"And you didn't think to tell me?"

"I told you everything you needed to know." He pauses and shakes his head disapprovingly. "Today, of all days," he mutters.

I frown. Today? What's so... oh. I should have remembered with the end of winter coming up. It's Ma's birthday. It's Ma's birthday, and I wasn't here. I've really messed up.

"Minnow, I think you should go."

"What? Go where?"

"That's up to you. Maybe go to those friends you spend so much time with. But if you don't want to respect me, and you don't want to be here for your Ma, then this place isn't right for you."

"Of course I want to be here for Ma," I object.

"And yet..." He doesn't finish his argument, but he doesn't need to. It's obvious. I haven't been here. He doesn't ask much of me at all, really: just to help Ma with lunch and her hair. And I've neglected all of my duties.

Shame engulfs me. But something else stirs in me, too: an ache for freedom. My whole life I've been tethered to this house, this family, the bakery. How much longer will my life continue in the same daily cycle? For how long will I have to endure the pain of seeing Ma float through each day without a single word or expression? Monotony. Exhaustion. Disappointment. That's all that awaits me in this household.

"Okay. I'll go."

I knock on Betty Gray's door as the sun finishes setting. Betty's eyes widen in surprise as she opens the door and sees me standing with a bag slung over my shoulder.

"I'm sorry to show up out of the blue," I say, "But I was wondering if I could stay here for a short while. If you have space." I know she has space – her house is the second largest in the village.

"Oh..." Her eyebrows draw together as a confused expression graces her wrinkled face. "Trouble at home?"

"Something like that."

She smiles. "Well, you're always welcome here, Minnow. I'm sure Cillian will be pleased to see you. Raina, too – she speaks so highly of you. Oh, but... she's not here, of course."

Raina speaks highly of me? I find that hard to believe.

Betty shows me to a spare room. Like most of the house, it is decorated with quilts, lace, and polished wooden furniture. And it smells like, well, old people.

"Stay as long as you need," says Betty. "We've eaten already, but there is some bread and butter on the kitchen bench you can help yourself to."

After I've unpacked the clothes I brought, I hear a gentle knock on my door.

"Come in," I call.

Cillian appears in the doorway. "What's happened, Minnow?"

I sigh. "Dad kicked me out."

Cillian scowls. "Do you want me to go and talk to him?"

"No. I think it's best if I give him space." I sit on the bed. Cillian takes a seat next to me.

"As sorry as I am for your situation, it's nice to see you," Cillian says. He places a warm hand on my leg.

"You too," I say.

Our eyes meet. My thigh suddenly feels hypersensitive to his touch. A tingle ripples through my body.

Slowly, he slides his hand up my thigh until his fingertips rest next to my crotch. I take his hand and press it into the space between my legs.

He runs his index finger over my slit. I lean in and kiss his lips. It feels like little explosions are erupting throughout my body. I need him.

I pull off my trousers and underwear. He takes off his clothes and stands before me in all his magnificence. I try not to stare at the shape hanging between his legs.

I take off my shirt and lay back on the bed. He lowers himself over me until his lips meet mine. His chest hair brushes against my bare breasts, tickling my nipples. He reaches down with his right hand and discovers how wet I am. He circles my clit with his finger, slowly at first, and then faster. Then, he shuffles down and sucks it. Just once. But it's enough to send a quiver through my whole body.

Next, he traces the tip of his tongue around my entrance, occasionally dipping it in and filling me with a soft warmth. He slides his tongue back along my slit and starts licking at my clit, flicking over it a few times before sucking it again. This time, he keeps sucking it. My heart is hammering in my chest and I can barely breathe properly. Just as I'm at the edge and think he's going to suck an orgasm out of me, he pulls away.

"I think you're ready for me now."

He slides on top of me, his warm chest pressed against mine. I can feel his hard dick against my leg. He pulls himself up and slowly eases himself inside me.

My hole eagerly stretches to take him in. If I could pull him in faster, I would – but he moves in ever-so-slowly. Every time I think he's in as deep as he can go, he slides in even further. All I can think about is how full of him I am. And how desperate I am for more.

I wrap my arms around his back. "Please. All the way in."

He slides in further, and finally his whole length is pressed inside me.

He starts moving out again, and I want to yell out in protest, but then he pushes back in and the bliss of the fullness returns. He keeps doing this: in and out, tickling something inside me that springs a wave of pleasure through me each time he rubs against it.

I hear myself gasping and moaning with each movement, even though I'm not making any sounds deliberately.

His thrusts quicken and my pulse beats in time.

"Cillian..." I moan.

"Minnow," he whispers in return. "My beloved Minnow."

I giggle. "You know it's the name of a fish, right?"

"It's also the name of the person most precious to me in all the world," he replies.

Bliss. Everything is bliss. Devotion in my bones and blood.

I wake up in Cillian's arms. I could lie here forever, nestled in safety and warmth. It is just past dawn, so I prod Cillian awake. He snuggles closer to me.

"You said we need to leave first thing," I remind him.

"Ugh, if you insist."

"You'd better get out before Betty realises you're in here."

After breakfast, we cross the bridge and head northeast to Walnut Woods. Flocks of chirping birds remind us that we are on the threshold of spring, with winter loosening its frosty grip.

I've never been to Yammoor, but I know from maps that it is right in the centre of the woods. We follow a dirt track designed for horse-drawn carts. When Yammoor comes into view, it is just as I imagined it: rows of solid log cabins, a single general store, and an empty town hall. Yammoor is even sleepier than Schlafhold. Its main exports are quality wood sourced from the surrounding forest and valuable ore from a nearby mine. Everyone is out at work, leaving the impression that the village is abandoned.

Cillian and I make our way to the store, figuring it will be the best place to find out more about the village's inhabitants. A stocky old man sits at the counter, surrounded by an array of wooden toys, clocks and pipes. He looks us up and down, clearly recognising that we are strangers to the village.

"Welcome to Yammoor," he says, although his tone is more wary than welcoming. "Can I interest you in a clock? They are all made locally."

"We're not after a clock, sorry," I say.

"Pity. Folks keep making them, but no-one wants to buy them." He stares at us for a few moments, and then continues. "What can I help you with?"

"We're looking for someone," I reply. "A... friend of ours. Abby."

"Ah, Abby. Well, she'll be out hunting, won't she?"

"Will she?" A woman's voice sounds from behind us. We turn and see Abby with a small deer carcass slung around her shoulders.

She appraises me. "You again."

Cillian speaks up. "We've come to ask for your help."

Abby raises her eyebrows. "Help with what?"

"Hunting something," I answer. "Something big."

Abby tilts her head to the side. "I'm listening."

I describe the serpent and briefly recount what happened when we faced it. The storekeeper's mouth drops open in shock.

Abby appears thoughtful. "What's in it for me?"

Cillian and I hesitate. We haven't thought about this. The pause weighs down awkwardly, and I can see Abby is already starting to lose interest.

"Bread," I pipe up. "As much bread as you want."

Abby studies me, appearing to consider this. Then, she tips back her head and roars with laughter. "Bread? Yammoor may be small, but we have our own bread. The baker lives just across the road."

I sigh, deflated. I don't know what else to offer.

"Name your price," Cillian says finally, crossing his arms.

Abby mirrors him. "I want a horse. A stallion. They have such beautiful horses in Schlafhold."

Cillian and I exchange glances. A horse?

"It's a deal," says Cillian.

CHAPTER 19

Haystack's brow furrows. "How long do you need to borrow him for?"

"Not borrow," I clarify, wrinkling my nose at the smell of horse manure. "We want to buy him."

Haystack strokes the rump of a tall black stallion, Midnight. "But what do you need a horse for? Where will you even keep it?"

"It's not technically for us," I admit. "It's a gift. For our friend in Yammoor."

"And who is this 'friend'? Do you trust them to take good care of Midnight? I don't sell my horses to just anybody."

I hesitate. While Abby seems like a decent person, I don't feel confident vouching for her. I barely know her!

Cillian has no such qualms. "She has my utmost respect and trust. I guarantee you, Midnight will be in good hands."

Haystack wrings his hands together nervously. He turns to me. "Minnow?"

"I..." I remember how important this is to Cillian's quest. "I agree with Cillian."

Haystack nods. "Alright then. He might have a better life elsewhere, anyway. Half of my lot have come down ill. Not sure why. Just a run of bad luck. Low-quality grass, maybe."

He hands over the stallion's reins. "Normally I'd charge eighty silver, but…" He flashes me a meaningful look. "Friends get half price."

My eyes widen. Forty silver is a hefty sum. That's about how much I earned in Harethorn.

Cillian produces a small pouch from his pocket. He places it in Haystack's hand. A tinkling sound rings out.

"That's fifty," states Cillian. "You can keep the change."

I stare at Cillian. I figured Betty must be rich, given the size of her house. So, by extension, it makes sense that Cillian would be well-off, too. But wealthy enough to carry around fifty silver in his pocket? It makes me uncomfortable, for some reason. What does he think of me, knowing that I have to scrape together every coin I can just to get by?

Haystack appears to be caught off-guard as well. "Th-thanks," he mutters.

I realise I still have a lot to learn about Cillian Gray. This man I've given my heart to, my body to… How many more mysteries does he hold?

Cillian heads for the stable exit, leading Midnight along.

As I turn, Haystack's soft hand gently encircles my wrist.

"Minnow…" he says quietly. "Promise me you won't go back to Haunted Lake."

I hold his gaze for a few moments and then slowly shake my head.

Haystack releases my arm, and the look of pain in his eyes is one I won't forget soon.

I drop by the apothecary to visit Raina before we are due to head back to Yammoor with the horse. When I arrive outside, Heron is chatting to Helix, who is propping himself up with a pair of crutches.

"You've adjusted well," Heron is saying. "Keep that bandage on until Monday."

Helix sees me and smiles. "Hi, Minnow."

"You look a lot better."

Helix manages to shrug one shoulder. "I'm just thankful to be here. Are you here to see your friend? She has been asking about you."

"She has?" I'm relieved to hear she is awake, and touched to know she's been thinking of me.

Helix chuckles. "Yes. She wanted to know all about you. She's quite the admirer. She said you tried to save her at... Haunted Lake." His voice goes quiet with the last words, and a forlorn look takes over his face.

An awkward silence ensues. I look away.

I expect Helix to scold me for going there, or to plead for me not to go back like Haystack did, but he says nothing.

"Take care," he says finally, and limps away.

I find Raina lying in a bed, tucked under white sheets. Her injured arm rests over her chest, still pale and streaked with black under the skin. She squints up at me before her face breaks into a smile.

"I was just complaining about how dark it is in here," she says. "But finally a ray of sunshine appears."

I want to ask her why she is being so nice to me all of a sudden – surely it's not just because I helped her? Perhaps she's delirious. In fact, that would make sense. Her eyelids flutter and her thin lips remain curved in a smile. Her eyes have a glazed look to them.

"How are you feeling?" I ask.

"Arm hurts," she mumbles.

"Yeah." I pull up a wooden chair and sit next to her. I notice a few strands of her dark hair are caught in her eyelashes. Without thinking, I reach down and guide them aside. Her skin is damp with sweat.

"Heron knows her stuff," declares Raina. "She used some very smelly herbs to slow the venom and wake me up."

"Slow the venom? Not cure it?"

Raina winces. "She's used the only antidote she has. But it's designed for your average forest-snakebite. Not the bite of a mega-humongous serpent of mythical proportions."

"So..."

"How long do I have left? Two, maybe three days."

I shake my head. "No. There has to be something else."

Raina reaches up with her good arm and touches my cheek with her knuckle. "Denial looks cute on you."

"How can you be so relaxed about this?!"

"Heron has given me a very high dose of... something. It's making me feel all fuzzy inside. But I figured I might as well accept my fate."

"Raina... you saved my life." My gaze meets hers. Those wise, secretive eyes twinkle back at me, pupils wide.

"Don't mention it," says Raina, waving her good arm dismissively.

"I won't let you die," I respond.

Raina sighs. "There's no point dwelling on it. There's only one thing that could help, but it's impossible."

I sit up straight. "What? What is it?"

"Have you heard of the Eleros flower?"

"No."

"Its nectar is used to treat venom and poisons. If anything could help, it would be Eleros nectar."

"A flower? That sounds doable."

Raina shakes her head. "They don't grow here."

"Okay, so where *do* they grow?"

"South."

"... How south?"

"Like... Twisted-infested forest south."

I gulp.

Raina smiles sadly. "That's right. Eleros flowers haven't been used for decades because they're so hard to get. I only know about them from my history books."

"What do they look like?"

"Minnow, you can't seriously-..."

"I'm just curious."

Raina rolls her eyes. "Medium-sized orange flower with pointed petals and a black stamen."

"Sounds easy to identify."

"Minnow..."

"I have to try, Raina."

"Don't. I forbid it. As your elder."

I laugh. "You're what? Twenty-five? At most?"

"I've got a few years on you."

"And you've got plenty more to come," I stand up.

"I would keep arguing, but I can barely stay awake," Raina moans, her eyelids starting to droop. "Don't throw your life away, Minnow. Or, if you have to, at least choose a better cause."

But as I look at her delicate features, black curls and dreamy expression, I can't imagine there being any better cause.

I'm going to save Raina.

CHAPTER 20

Outside Betty's house, Cillian stands with his hands on his hips, eyebrows raised. "No way. You told me yourself – the southern forest is filled with Twisteds."

"You don't have to come with me." I shrug. "I can be fast, and I can be quiet. All I have to do is find a flower. Then I'll come straight back."

"It's far too dangerous."

"You say that all the time, about everything. But I'm still here. So are you. And I'm here because of Raina. I have to try and save her."

"But... the Curse. We're so close. I just need the stones..."

"The Curse can wait, can't it? Raina's life is on the line!"

Cillian stares at me. It's a hard, steely look. I can tell a dozen thoughts are racing through his head, but he holds his tongue.

I continue, "I'm going tonight. Raina doesn't have much time left."

Cillian grits his teeth. "It's foolish, Minnow. I'm not risking my life for this."

"She's your cousin!"

"Yes, but I also have a son! A son who needs me alive. He's why I'm here. Every choice I've made, every risk I've taken, has been so I can be reunited with him. He matters more to me than anything else."

His words hang in the air.

Of course his son matters more to him than anything else. Parents are supposed to love their children above everything. But I feel a smidgen of jealousy. *I* want to matter to him more than anything else.

"Fine," I say. "I'll go alone."

"You won't make it, Minnow. Twisteds show no mercy. You barely know how to wield your blade. You're no good at fighting. And you're not agile."

His blunt response stuns me. His expression remains firm, refusing to bend into an apology. Maybe he doesn't see a need to apologise.

Maybe he's right.

I'm not good at fighting. I could never beat a Twisted in battle.

"And let's face it," Cillian goes on. "You're not exactly a great runner, either."

"Any more comments on my fitness?"

"I meant because of your breathing. I've noticed you struggle."

"I suppose you've noticed I'm fat, too?" It's the first time in years that I've felt insecurity about my size emerging from the depths. It's a wretched feeling which leaves muddy footprints all over my insides. But suddenly I feel scrutinised in Cillian's eyes. What other flaws does he see in me? I want to fold in on myself, to retreat into my shell like a snail.

"I'm not trying to offend you," Cillian says softly. "I'm just looking out for you. Anyway, I need your help at Haunted Lake."

"Why? I barely know how to wield my blade. I'm no good at fighting. I'm not agile. I can't even run properly. I don't see how I can be of any use to you."

Cillian steps closer to me, reaching for my hand. "Forget what I said, Minnow. I didn't mean it."

I pull away. "Yes, you did. You always think about what you're saying. It's something I like about you." The urge to cry tunnels up my throat. "Do you think I don't have any self-respect? That I'll just sit back and let you talk that way about me?"

"No. You're right. I shouldn't have said it. I just wanted you to stay..."

"Alright then. I'll stay. But not with you."

I push past him through Betty's front door and grab my bag from my room. "I'm going to see Thivya." It's a lie. I'm heading south. But I know that if Cillian realises this, he'll try to stop me.

"Minnow, please," Cillian begs as I head back out the door.

I ignore him.

"Minnow, I just want you to be safe. Minnow, I..."

"You what?" I turn and stare at him.

His mouth hangs open, but he doesn't say anything.

For a moment I wonder if he was going to say he loves me. What would I do then? Would I forgive him? The idea of him telling me he loves me launches butterflies through my body, despite the anger I feel. Or am I just craving validation now that he's managed to unstack the blocks of self-esteem I've built up over the years?

"I think I need a break from you, Cillian," I murmur.

With that, I walk away.

The threat of Twisteds has always deterred me from travelling far beyond the treeline to the south, despite the fact that the Twisteds are so far away that none have been sighted this far north in decades. The idea of them alone is enough to keep anyone away. How far will I need to go before I find an Eleros flower? Hours? Days? I remember that Raina doesn't have much time left, and I plunge forwards into the darkness.

I hold a tiny lantern in front of me. It casts just enough light to illuminate chunky tree roots that threaten to trip me if I take my eyes off the ground. After a few hours, every shadow at the corner of my vision signals danger. The wings of a swooping owl. A broken branch swinging limply from a tree. Clouds passing momentarily over the moon. I feel so small, surrounded by a forest which, as far as I know, stretches to the end of the world.

The sound of a twig snapping underfoot splits the silence. I whip out my protection knife. The silver tip of the blade catches a beam of moonlight.

I look around, wide-eyed, straining to see in the darkness. Is that a shape moving up ahead? No, it's just a rock. I rub my eye with the back of my hand, careful not to stab myself.

I'm convinced there is something out there. Off to the right, where the snapping sound came from. Lowering my feet ever-so-softly onto the ground as I walk, I slowly follow the direction of the sound.

A small clearing in the trees becomes visible. I hold up my lamp. There, standing in the middle of the clearing, is a huge stag. It lowers its antlered head and sniffs the ground.

I sigh with a mixture of awe and relief. The creature is so sleek, so smooth. I want to reach out my hand and touch its short, silver-brown hair.

Suddenly, something crashes into the clearing with a screech. It grabs onto the stag by the throat, burying its face in his fur.

A Twisted.

The stag tosses its head wildly and attempts to bolt, but the Twisted keeps a firm grip on the stag's neck with its teeth and claws. To my alarm, the stag begins trotting in my direction, dragging the Twisted with it.

I stagger backwards and hide behind a tree, dropping my lantern in the process. It makes a *clink* noise as it collides with a tree root and shatters. There is a burst of flame which is quickly extinguished by a gust of wind.

Now I only have moonlight to guide my way.

I wait until the sounds of the stag and the Twisted have faded away. For a moment I forget why I'm out here – the whole situation seems so preposterous. Alone in the southern forest in the middle of the night. Barely able to see two feet in front of me. In Twisted territory.

I wonder what their sense of smell is like. Can they track humans by their scent? I'm increasingly aware of the sour sweat coating my brow. Anxious sweat made cold by the wind.

I stumble onwards through the forest. I keep my left hand out in front of me to feel for any unexpected obstructions. My right hand still grips my knife.

Occasionally I notice signs that Twisteds have passed: scratch marks on tree bark, deep footprints and scuffs in the dirt, a rabbit carcass with its innards ripped out.

Although I need to focus on my surroundings, Cillian's words from earlier echo in my mind. Has he always looked down on me? Does he feel blinded by my blazing incompetence?

And yet, haven't I held my own? I've escaped pirates, dodged a griffin, and solved the mystery of Haunted Lake. Maybe I didn't land any killing blows, but I survived. I'm not just the baker's daughter anymore.

As I wander on, a sickly sweet smell assaults my senses. A floral smell. Raina didn't mention the Eleros flower having a scent, but how would she know? She said she only knew about it from her history books.

I kneel down and start crawling. The last thing I want to do is trample the flower in the dark. I follow my nose. The smell is so strong that it is almost repulsive. Finally, sprouting out of the ground in front of me is a delicate plant with pale, broad flowers. It is hard to tell their colour in the dim light, but based on the fact that they are the only flowers I have seen, I have to trust that they are what I am looking for.

I snap a few flowers from their stems. Sticky sap clings to my fingers. I gently place the flowers in my pocket. The odour is even more intense now. I wipe my fingers on the edge of my cloak, although the stickiness remains. Ugh. Time to go home.

I try to head back exactly the way I came, but it's hard to find a non-existent path in the dark. Bushes and thick foliage block my way. I think I drift slightly east, still forging my way north as directly as possible. A harsh croaking sound makes me pause. It makes me think of a frog being throttled. But it's much more powerful, and undoubtedly emanates from a Twisted.

I stand as still as possible as I determine the direction of the sound. As I strain to listen, I realise there are other sounds I didn't notice before, too: hissing and a low humming.

I know I should get as far away from here as possible, but I'm worried that if I deviate from my path then I will get lost in the forest. Tentatively, I continue forwards, cringing every time my footsteps make a sound.

The strange noises grow louder. The ground beneath me becomes harder, and I realise I'm on a sheaf of rock overhanging a ditch. I'll have to double back and find a way around, because I don't fancy leaping over the edge and risking broken bones. All the same, I go up to the lip of the rock and look down into the ditch below.

Huddled in a group are at least a dozen Twisteds. They all stand shoulder-to-shoulder in a circle facing each other, emitting guttural cries, deep growls and sharp hisses. They all appear to be trembling slightly, as if vibrating. It's a bizarre sight. Every now and then, one of them will toss its head back and let out a mighty screech, and the others follow suit. I wonder what the purpose of this group ritual is. Bonding? Competition? I can't tell.

A shiver suddenly runs through my body.

I've never understood when people describe feeling like they're being watched. I assumed it was just an expression, or an embellishment added after the fact, or some bizarre sixth sense I don't possess.

But I feel it now. It's like my skin is crawling, like there's something settled on my back and I want to shake it off. A faint nausea flutters through my stomach and chest.

I scan the group of Twisteds, but none of them have noticed me. All the same, I decide to back away from the ledge. My heel catches on something as I step backwards, and I topple onto my behind. I let out an involuntary gasp as I hit the ground.

Oh no.

The Twisteds fall silent. In fact, the whole forest goes silent. I hold my breath.

I inch myself forwards so that I can just see over the edge of the rock into the ditch below. The Twisteds are all facing my direction, listening with cocked heads. One of them spots me and lets out a screech, its yellow eyes widening. The others erupt into similar calls and noises. They lunge in my direction, but are unable to scale the rock face. A couple of them break away from the pack to search for a way up. I'm really in for it now.

There is a sudden sound like the beat of a heart, but loud and echoey. The Twisteds stop making noise. I look down and see them begin to writhe, each of them contorting on the spot, appearing to shrivel up and... shrink? I watch in shock as they morph into... trees. Wonky, leafless trees. Soon, all of the Twisteds have transformed into trees and the forest becomes utterly still.

"You're welcome," comes a voice from behind me.

I pivot on the spot.

There, standing stock-still among the trees, is a short figure wearing a hooded cloak that covers most of her body. Her dark eyes are just visible beneath the shadow of her hood. Her lip is slightly curled up on the left side, as if she is amused.

A Witch.

She looks old, and yet there isn't a single blemish or wrinkle on her face.

"You did that?" I ask, although the answer is obvious.

"Did you find what you're looking for?" Her voice is clear as a bell, but her mouth doesn't move as she speaks. There is a slight echo to the words, as if they are spoken within a tree hollow.

I nod.

"You carry good luck," she remarks, again not moving her lips. "May it grant you safe passage." She pauses, then, "Don't come back here."

With that, she turns and slinks away into the forest.

My heart is hammering. Why is she out wandering the forest so late at night? Or is that just what Witches do? I cast a glance back at where the Twisteds were. Still trees.

As I begin my journey back to Schlafhold, I am preoccupied with questions about Witches. Where do they come from? Were they once ordinary women, or were they born

Witches? Were they born at all, or did they come into being some other way? Are they all the same, or are there different types of Witches with different powers? Maybe Raina has some answers from her studies.

My heart rate quickens at the thought of Raina. Her warmth, her wry laughter, her easy smile... I long to see her again.

The feeling is unexpected. Doesn't she annoy me? Doesn't she get in the way of me having time alone with Cillian? And yet... I feel connected to her. And not just because she saved my life.

The sun rises. The warm beams are a relief for my icy cold hands. I press on through the forest. The trees begin to thin, and I realise I'm almost home. I've made it out of Twisted territory.

I head straight for the apothecary and procure the flowers from my pocket. Sturdy orange blooms.

I rap on Heron's door. She opens it clumsily, trying to gather her hair into her headscarf at the same time.

She looks at me, confused, and then sees the bundle of flowers in my hand.

"Oh, Minnow... I'm so sorry. You're too late."

CHAPTER 21

Heron leads me to Raina's bed.

Raina is lying still, her head lolled to one side. I stare down at her lifeless body and get the sensation that I'm free-falling, as if the floor has disappeared from underneath me.

"It's been peaceful," explains Heron. "She fell asleep late in the night. Betty and Cillian have already said their goodbyes."

I reach out and take Raina's hand. It's still warm.

"She's not dead!" I cry, almost dropping her hand in surprise.

"She doesn't have long left," says Heron. "The venom has spread throughout her whole body. She's barely breathing."

I thrust the Eleros flowers in Heron's direction. "These can cure her. She told me so."

Heron shakes her head. "Even if I prepared the nectar, she would need to drink it. But she's not conscious. She won't wake up."

I shake my head. "We have to try."

Heron just stares at me sadly.

"Heron, please!" I clutch at my hair. "Please."

"I don't want to get your hopes up…"

"My heart is filled with hope," I argue. "She can only be saved with hope."

Heron presses her lips together. After a moment of hesitation, she takes the flowers from me.

I sit by Raina's side and stroke her hair as Heron prepares the nectar.

"Please stay," I whisper into Raina's ear. She doesn't react. She has become alarmingly pale, a stark contrast to the feverish flush she had the last time I saw her. The colour has drained from her lips.

Heron brings over a wooden goblet containing the nectar. I shuffle aside so that Heron can reach Raina. As I move, something brushes against my leg. I reach into my pocket and wrap my fingers around its contents: the little wooden horse Haystack gave me.

You carry good luck.

Haystack said it brought him luck, didn't he? And I just emerged unscathed from the depths of the southern forest. That had to be luck.

I press the horse into Raina's palm and hold her fingers around it.

Heron holds the goblet of nectar up to Raina's lips. Raina's mouth doesn't open, so Heron uses her index finger to prise Raina's lips apart and tip the nectar in.

I watch in silence. At first, there is no response from Raina. Then, she coughs, tossing her head forwards and back. Her fingers tighten around the wooden horse.

Unable to move, I watch as Raina convulses. Wheezing sounds emanate from her throat. Her back arches.

"Is she okay?" I ask, turning to Heron.

Heron says nothing.

Raina's eyes fly open, and she suddenly sits bolt upright. She gasps, swallows, and gasps again.

"Raina..." I say, taking her hand in both of mine.

She looks around the room wildly before her gaze settles on me. "Minnow..."

"I'm here. It's okay. You're okay." I wrap her in a hug.

Heron shakes her head in disbelief. "I didn't think it was possible."

Raina unfurls her fingers to reveal the wooden horse. Its pointed ears and outstretched legs have left red indents in her skin. "What's this?"

"A lucky charm," I reply. "I think it saved you."

Raina shakes her head. "You saved me."

Our eyes meet. Her gaze is welcoming, daring. It pulls me in, willing me to be closer to her.

"I should let you rest," I say at last, breaking away.

"Stay," pleads Raina weakly.

So, I shuffle my chair closer and hold her hand as she rests and the colour slowly returns to her face.

I wake with my head on an unusual pillow, which I soon realise is Raina's chest. One of her arms rests over me, as if I am a child's toy she is holding close.

Her warmth seeps into me. My warmth circles back to her. I feel at peace.

Hours pass. I drift in and out of sleep.

Finally, Raina stirs with a groan.

"Hey," she mumbles.

"Hey," I respond, sitting up. "How are you feeling?"

"I feel… fine," she marvels. She holds up her injured arm. The black streaks have gone, leaving only two scabs where the fang-marks were. "In fact, I feel more alive than ever." She pokes me. "You look like you need a few more hours of sleep."

I rub my eyes wearily and feel how puffy they are. "Hey, if I'd gone to bed on time, you wouldn't be alive."

"I know," says Raina, "And you look gorgeous anyway." Her smile is bold, and yet there is a fragility to it.

"You've been so much nicer to me since Haunted Lake," I remark. "I really thought you didn't like me."

"I guess I was a bit jealous."

"Because of Cillian? Raina, he's your cousin!"

"Not jealous of *you*. Jealous of *him*. Jealous he had you all to himself."

"Well… he doesn't anymore."

Raina fixes me with her gaze, as if waiting. There it is again. The daring invitation. I lean in closer to her, realising how much I miss her warmth. How much I want to press my skin against hers. How much I want to kiss her…

Her lips are soft like the first rays of dawn.

She draws away and stares at me as if she has never seen anything like me.

I feel giddy, and a little wobbly. It's not a bad feeling, as such… but it sets me off-balance.

"You… you must be hungry," I stammer. "I'll go get you something to eat." Before Raina has time to say anything else, I pull on my cloak and hurry out the door.

The air is humid. I wonder if a storm is on the way. I stroll down the main street of the village. My instinct is to go to the bakery, but I'm not ready to see Dad – and I doubt he's ready to see me.

I pass Mr Gust's miscellaneous goods shop, and the mural on the wall catches my eye. It looks even better in the light of day. Someone has added a yellow sun in the top left. I spot the hand prints left by Cillian and I, down in the bottom corner. Thumbs touching. It unsettles me now. In that moment, he had seemed perfect to me. Our passion had felt like something that would last forever. Was I naive to have thought that? And now, the feelings for Raina which sneaked up on me – is it foolish of me to give credence to them?

And yet, maybe it's exactly what I need. A slice of something else, an insight into another possibility. Paint over the heartbreak. It would take my mind off Cillian, at least. So... maybe I should lean into it.

I return to Raina with a punnet of fresh strawberries from the grocer. She eagerly gobbles up the berries. Once she has finished and has licked the red juice off her lips, she turns to me.

"Where's Heron?"

"She's out visiting the elderly villagers at this time of day," I answer.

Raina nods. "So, it's just you and me."

"That's right. Just us."

"I liked when you were close to me." She pulls me towards her, onto the bed.

I hesitate.

Raina notices, and the corner of her mouth curls up empathically. "Sorry... maybe this is too much for you. I mean, with Cillian and everything."

"No," I say. "I don't want to think about Cillian."

Raina touches my cheek with the tip of her finger. "Will you share a moment with me, then?"

I nod. My heart rate speeds up. The ache I feel to be close to her overpowers my doubt.

Raina slowly, tenderly pulls my shirt over my head and casts it aside. She runs her warm hand over my exposed breasts, causing my nipples to stand on end.

"You're so beautiful," she whispers.

She takes off her own shirt, then the rest of her clothes as well so she is sitting next to me entirely naked. Everything about her body looks perfect. Almost too perfect. I gingerly reach out and trace the sharp line of her collarbone, and then lean in and kiss it.

As I kiss her, she presses herself against me. A gasp escapes her lips as I plant a line of kisses along her collarbone and then all the way up her neck. She grabs my hair at the back of my head and squeezes slightly. It feels good.

Raina slides a hand down my side and then tugs at my pants until they slide off. Raina's hand glosses over my leg until it rests on my upper thigh.

"I want you," she says. "I've wanted you ever since I first saw you." She leans in to kiss me on the lips. I kiss her back. She tastes sweet, like grape juice. She moves and kisses my chin, then my throat, and then kisses a line down my chest, between my breasts and all the way to my belly button. Then she turns her attention to my left breast and begins tracing around it with her tongue.

I quiver at the sensation. I reach down and take her own breast in my hand, massaging it gently. Hers feels firmer than mine, and it's coated in an almost-invisible layer of dark hair.

I can feel a slickness between my legs, and it is comforting knowing that I am able to feel just as turned on by a woman. I had been worried that maybe I was wrong. I don't know any other girls who are attracted to women. I've often wondered whether it's normal for everyone, but no-one has ever mentioned it. But here, with Raina in my arms, I know it's real. And I want it.

Raina comes up and kisses my lips again. I gently roll her onto her side and then reach down to the curly bush between her thighs. I explore it slowly, running my fingertip over the black curls, over the lips, until sinking it into the wet opening that I know is waiting for me.

Raina gasps and grips onto my upper arm. She closes her eyes. I keep kissing her as I stroke along her crevice. She squirms a little and grips me tighter each time I pass my finger over her clit.

"I want..." she gasps, "I want to touch you."

"Okay." I smile.

Her hand goes to my vulva, and she begins stroking circles around my clit. It feels like a bolt of lightning shoots through my body. I buck my hips, pressing into her.

"Yes..." I moan.

"Can I kiss you there?" she whispers.

I nod.

Seconds later, Raina is suckling on my clit. She moans in delight, sending vibrations throughout my body. I feel my clit swelling in size within the warm cocoon of her mouth. Each time she sucks it, it feels as if there is a wave of water crashing at a flood wall, trying to break through. Then it ebbs away again, before inevitably being drawn back. She starts to tease my enlarged bauble with the tip of her tongue, each stroke sending a wave of pleasure through me. Then she sucks on it once more, as if she is sucking the pulp from an orange.

"Ah..." I cry out. I'm right on the edge. Pressure builds up in my crotch and chest. My leg begins to quiver and I come, my clit pulsating between Raina's lips.

Moments later, I do the same for her.

Raina pulls her clothes back on. "I don't do long-term commitments. Just so you know."

"So, this was a one-time thing?"

"Maybe not *one*-time," she responds, with a twinkle in her eye. "But I'm not staying in Schlafhold long. I don't want you to get the wrong idea."

"I'll miss you if you go."

She smiles. "Don't know if anyone's ever said that to me before."

There is a sharp rapping on the door. "Raina?!"

It's Cillian.

I quickly finish dressing as Cillian bursts into the room. His eyes widen as he sees Raina sitting up.

"I thought you were dead," he gasps, rushing to her side.

"Not yet," grins Raina. "Thanks to Minnow."

Cillian stares at me in disbelief. "You did it? You got the flower?"

"No need to sound so shocked," I retort.

Cillian turns his attention back to Raina. "How do you feel?"

"Fantastic," says Raina, smirking in my direction. "I've had one of the best mornings ever."

I try to hide my guilty smile.

"I'm so relieved you're okay," says Cillian. "Do you think... do you think you'll come back to Haunted Lake with us?"

My jaw drops open, as does Raina's.

"What?" demands Raina. "Are you mad?"

"We need all the help we can get," insists Cillian. He speaks quickly, as if possessed by an overwhelming urgency.

"Now is not the time, Cillian," I argue. "She's just been through a massive ordeal. And you want her to go back to the place where she was almost killed?"

Cillian takes a deep breath as if preparing an argument in return, but he holds it in. Finally, he gives in. "Fine. You're right. I'm sorry. I just... I just want this all to be over."

Now I can see how much exhaustion is weighing him down. Circles are beginning to form under his eyes. His skin has a greyish tinge to it. His lips are dry.

"I just want to see my boy," he murmurs.

My heart breaks for him as tears well up in his eyes.

"I'll come with you," I say. "It's safer with more people. But Raina stays here."

"I can speak for myself, thank you," Raina butts in. "But yes. I'm staying right here."

Cillian nods. "Okay. Thank you, Minnow."

Cillian's scent reaches me: that deep, tranquil forest glen. I can't help but feel drawn to it. And without meaning to, I find myself remembering what it felt like when he... when he...

I dig my nails into my palm to snap myself out of it. You're annoyed with him, remember, Minnow? You chose to break it off.

Raina holds the wooden horse out to me. "Be careful, Minnow." Unnoticed by Cillian, she puckers her lips and sends a kiss in my direction.

CHAPTER 22

Once I know Dad is busy in the bakery, I sneak into the cottage in search of Ma. Rather than finding her seated by the window, I see she is tucked in bed. Beads of sweat dot her brow. She still has a fever.

I sit on the bed next to her and place a hand on her arm. Her eyes remain closed.

"Remember when you called my name?" I ask her. "I heard you. I came straightaway." I touch a strand of her jet-black hair. "I'm sorry I haven't been here. I just have to go away one last time, and then I'll be back for good." I hesitate, then, "But if you ask me to stay, I'll stay." I wait. It feels like a trick, but deep down I know she can't hear me anyway.

A surge of missing her passes through me. I miss going on picnics together, doing our hair together, cooking together, laughing together. I miss her. Her joy, her wit, her gentleness. I feel the weight of losing her. I feel it again and again, and yet in some ways I haven't lost her at all. She's still here in front of me, isn't she? It feels wrong to grieve the living.

I kiss her on the forehead and whisper goodbye. As always, I secretly hope that the next time I see her, she'll be back to how she used to be, as if that life-changing day never happened. As if it was just a mistake the universe made which has finally been corrected.

Abby's hair is tied up in a tight bun. She is dressed in animal skins and a fur jacket, like a true hunter. A multitude of feathered arrows sit in a quiver on her back. Our lives may very well depend on those arrows.

"Let's get this over and done with," Abby says grimly, just as it starts to rain.

The path to Haunted Lake quickly becomes muddy. Specks of mud splash onto the hems of my trouser legs. Water collects in my hair. I look to Cillian to see if he is considering turning back, but his face is fixed with a look of determination.

Wet clothing clings to my skin as we arrive at Haunted Lake. The village's usual eerie silence is disrupted by rain hammering down on wood, stone and earth, as well as the occasional rumble of thunder high above us. I wish I wasn't here.

Cillian plants himself firmly on the spot where the serpent attacked us last time. The body of the Twisted has gone – the serpent must have eaten it.

Cillian looks around, blinking through raindrops. "Come out!" he calls. "We're here!"

His voice is drowned out by the rain. Pools of water collect in our muddy footprints. I wrap my arms around my body, pressing my cold limbs against my chest.

"We have to make the ground shake," advises Abby. "That's how snakes detect predators and prey. They sense vibrations in the earth."

The last thing I want to do is jump in the mud and send splatters everywhere, but Cillian is already doing it. Abby looks on, appraising him and then deciding she will let him do the hard work.

I stomp on the ground a few times tentatively, wincing as the ground squishes beneath my boot. "Maybe it doesn't like water!" I call out.

Cillian clenches his fists in frustration.

Then I see it.

About one hundred paces away, slithering at high speed in our direction, unhindered by the mud.

"There!" I cry.

Abby has already drawn her bow and arrow. She squints as she takes aim at the creature. "You made it sound bigger," she remarks. She lets loose the arrow. It reaches the serpent but glances off its scales. She fires another one, but once again it clips the serpent's back before bouncing away. The serpent wriggles aside slightly, but doesn't slow.

"It's going to kill us," I murmur under my breath as the serpent continues to charge in our direction. I start to back away. Torrents of rain cascade down all around me.

"Minnow," instructs Abby. "I need you to stand right here, in front of me."

Right in the serpent's path? "No way."

"I need you to trust me," insists Abby.

I hardly know her! But her voice has a firm, confident quality to it. I'm inclined to obey...

I look over and see Cillian poised with his protection knife in hand, gaze fixed on the serpent.

I might as well make myself useful. I do as Abby says, standing ahead of her in the serpent's path. A shiver passes through me as I see the creature's keen black eyes locked on me. Its head rises from the ground, mouth opening, ready to strike...

An arrow zips past me through the air, surging forwards before lodging itself in the serpent's mouth.

The serpent recoils sharply. Abby fires another arrow, which strikes the serpent's right eye.

As the creature bucks its head, Cillian charges forwards and sinks his blade into the serpent's neck. The knife pierces the flesh beneath the scales.

Abby fires one more arrow into the serpent's mouth. The serpent raises its head in the air one last time and then flops onto the ground, dead.

We all watch in silence for a moment. Rain as cold as death trickles under the neck of my shirt and down my back, causing my spine to tingle.

"You did it," I say at last.

"Thank you, Abby," says Cillian. "And thank you, Minnow."

"Anytime," says Abby. "I'll be off now. Don't want to be late for dinner."

She turns on her heel and departs.

Cillian washes serpent-blood off his knife in a puddle of water, and then turns his attention to the lake. The surface of the dark water dances as droplets of rain patter across it.

"It's too cold, Cillian," I say. "You'll get sick if you swim in it now. It's bad enough that we're soaked through with rain. If you go in that water, you might not come out."

"But we're here," he argues. "We've fought so hard for this." He takes a deep breath. "I'm going in."

He walks to the pier and kicks off his boots.

"Cillian," I plead. "Think about this. You'll be soaking wet, and you won't be able to get warm again. Unless..."

"Unless?"

I look to the abandoned buildings. "I'll get a fire going. That hut's roof is still intact. Find me under there when you're done."

Cillian nods. Then, he turns and dives into Haunted Lake.

I rush over to the abandoned hut, knowing that I don't have long. Luckily, there is enough dry wood and scraps of paper on the floor to provide kindling for a fire. I stack the wood in the corner and after a few minutes I have a small fire blazing.

I poke my head out of the doorway and see Cillian's head above the water for a moment, before he sucks in a lungful of air and ducks back under. It must be near-impossible to see anything under that water. I'd assumed that the stones coated the floor of the lake, but what if there are only a few of them, hidden among the depths?

My clothes stick to my skin uncomfortably, so I elect to take off my shirt, socks and trousers and lay them by the fire to dry. It's not as if anyone is going to see me. Besides Cillian, that is, and it's not anything he hasn't seen before.

Cillian emerges a few minutes later, sopping wet and shivering. His fist is clenched. He unfurls it to reveal three small, black stones.

I grin at him. He forces a smile back through chattering teeth.

"What a treat to feast my eyes on," he says, his eyes roaming my bare skin.

I feel my cheeks sting with heat as I blush.

"I suppose I should do the same," he decides, taking off his clothes. Unlike me, he takes off his underwear too, letting his manhood dangle free. I try not to stare, feigning a sudden keen interest in a hole in the wall.

Cillian kneels in front of the fire and sucks in a sharp breath of air between his teeth as his body is wracked with shivering.

"Do you feel okay?" I ask.

"I feel a little faint, if I'm being honest," he replies. "Floaty."

"Give me your hands," I say. He holds his hands out to me and I grasp them in mine. They are clammy, wrinkled and ice cold to the touch. I squeeze them softly, hoping that some of my warmth will transfer to him.

"You're so kind to me, Minnow," he whispers. "I don't deserve all the help you've given me. Not after what I said to you." He looks at me with those soft hazel eyes. "I should never have doubted you. You've proven again and again that you are strong and capable of amazing things. You're special, Minnow." He raises my hands to his lips and kisses them.

"Not enough people in your life appreciate that. But you're so, so special."

Again, I think, that's why I fall for Cillian. He sees me, really sees me, and he regards me as something more than the boring baker's daughter who lives an ordinary life in a sleepy village. He recognises that I am capable of so much more. I *am* brave. I *am* strong. I *am* useful. I *do* try hard. And Cillian appreciates it.

All the warm feelings for him that I've suppressed bubble to the surface again. I think he senses it, because he kisses my hands again and then slowly plants a line of kisses up my right arm, gently pulling me closer to him in the process. When he reaches my shoulder, he rests his chin there and tilts my face to face him.

"Being apart from you made me realise how drastic a mistake I made," he confesses. "Because the truth is... I love you, Minnow."

He loves me. My heart skips. He wraps his arm around my back and holds me close as he kisses me on the lips. His bare skin presses against mine and we kiss and kiss. It feels like my insides are dissolving into a warm flood of excitement. The sound of the rain outside fades away and all I can hear is my heartbeat and his breath.

His hand slides down my body towards the crevice between my legs. My skin tingles at his touch. I mirror his hand's path on his own body, tracing his skin lower and lower...

His cock is thick and bulging. I cup my hand over the tip of it and feel its weight. The heaviness in my hand makes my groin throb with longing.

Despite the desperate ache I feel, I waver for a moment. I don't feel guilty, but I still feel uncomfortable with the idea of not telling Cillian about Raina. I pull away from him.

Cillian looks concerned, his eyebrows drawing together. "What's wrong? Are you alright?"

"There's something I should tell you," I say, taking a deep breath.

"What is it?"

"When you and I were on a break... I spent some time with someone else."

He blinks, and then looks at me expectantly.

The words are harder to get out than I thought they would be, like balls of wool pushing their way through my mouth. "It was Raina. I... you know. With Raina."

Cillian's jaw drops open. "With Raina?! Minnow-..."

"I know, I know, she's your cousin. I'm sorry."

Cillian shakes his head. "Raina's not my cousin. Raina is my grandmother."

I scoff. "What?"

"Raina is my grandmother."

I stare at him, waiting for him to break into laughter at his joke. But his face remains a mixture of shock and horror.

"What..." I stammer. "What do you mean she's your *grandmother*?"

"Raina made a deal with a Witch. Shortly after she gave birth to my mother. She was desperate not to grow old. So, the Witch put a Spell of eternal youth on her. A Blessing, or maybe a Curse. No doubt she had some price to pay for it."

"But... why didn't you tell me?"

"I had no idea you would try and sleep with her!" exclaims Cillian. "There was no reason for you or anyone in the village to know. It's much easier to say that we're cousins. Raina doesn't need everyone knowing her private history."

My chest burns with feelings of betrayal. I can't be angry at Cillian – if anyone should have told me, it's Raina. She tricked me.

Before I have time to further think through the implications, a gust of wind billows through the open doorway of the hut, causing the fire to shudder. More alarming is the sound carried by the wind: a thin, drawn-out whistle.

"That wasn't just the wind, was it?" says Cillian warily.

"I don't think so."

I feel my body tensing up as another harsh whistle rings through the air, this time unaccompanied by wind.

"Twisteds," growls Cillian, grasping at his clothes and quickly dressing. I do the same.

Cillian peeks out the doorway, squinting as he tries to peer through a deluge. "I don't think they're close. Maybe in the forest to the southeast."

"We should get back home as soon as possible." A sickening realisation dawns on me. "You don't think... You don't think the Twisteds have been living at the edge of the forest all along? And the only thing keeping them away was the serpent?"

Cillian's mouth opens slowly.

"Which means," I continue, "That they could reach Schlafhold next." I clench my fists. "We have to warn everyone."

I make for the door, but Cillian grabs my arm.

"Wait," he says. "I'm not going back."

"What do you mean? You've got the stones. You have everything you need to create the Counterspell!"

"That's exactly it. I have everything I need with me now. There's no reason for me to return to Schlafhold."

"But... what about me? Won't you be with me?"

"Ah yes, you." He cups my cheek in his hand and leans in. "I do need you." Then, he slips his protection knife out from its sheath and runs the blade along my forearm, creating a bloody gash.

CHAPTER 23

I shriek in pain and shock. The wound isn't deep, but a line of blood forms and trickles down the side of my arm.

Before I can wrap my head around what is happening, Cillian produces a small, round glass vial from his pocket and holds the opening to my arm, collecting the blood. I tear my arm away and hold it to my chest.

"What are you doing?!" I demand, my voice an octave higher than usual.

Cillian raises the vial to eye-height and swirls its contents around. My blood.

Cillian sighs. "There was another ingredient I never told you about. One last thing to check off the list." He places a stopper in the vial and pockets it. "Blood of the devoted."

"The devoted?"

"I needed you to be devoted to me," he responds with a shrug of his shoulders.

"I'm not *devoted* to you," I argue, feeling a little insulted.

"And yet you have risked your life for me, repeatedly."

I search his face for a flicker of warmth, and inkling of care, but his eyes are cold and stern.

"Was this your plan all along?" I ask. "Trick me into falling in love with you, just so you could use me? Do you even like me?"

Cillian sighs again. "I wouldn't have chosen you if I didn't see something in you."

How many times can my heart be broken in one day? First I find out Raina deceived me, and now this. An even greater deception.

I feel naked, even though I'm fully clothed. Naked, fragile, hurt. I look down at my arm, noticing a red stain spreading on my shirt where I've clutched it to my chest.

"The wound is shallow enough to close itself," Cillian advises. "You won't need stitches. Give it a few minutes."

"Don't talk to me," I say. "I don't want to hear anything else from you."

A flicker of hurt graces Cillian's face. "This wasn't easy, Minnow. I..." He chokes up a little. Real emotion? Or just part of the act he's been keeping up? "I wouldn't do this if I didn't truly have to."

"Get away from me." My bottom lip quivers.

"So be it." He turns and exits the hut, stepping into the rain which is finally beginning to ease.

Another harsh whistle pierces the air, and I'm reminded that I need to leave, too. Cradling my arm to my chest, I step out into the abandoned village. I look in the direction of the forest and, to my horror, see at least a dozen figures moving between the trees. A horde of Twisteds. If they head in this direction, it will only be a few hours before they reach Schlafhold.

I stagger back west in the direction of home, slowed by my painful arm and the weight of a shattered heart. Now that I'm alone, tears stream down my cheeks and mingle with the sprinkling of rain on my face. I let out unabashed, hearty sobs. When I finally thought someone loved me, they were lying all along. This is worse than never being loved at all.

And yet, I have been loved, haven't I? Just not by Cillian. My people love me – Dad, Thivya, Haystack, Heron, all the townsfolk who stop by the bakery and greet me each day. A love I've taken for granted. In the case of Dad, a love I've rejected in favour of the mirage offered by Cillian.

What a mistake I've made.

The dirt track leading back to Schlafhold has been completely muddied by the rain and in many places drowned in puddles of deep water. I find myself drifting away from the path to avoid ending up shin-deep in brown water. At first I think this is a better idea anyway, as I can cut through the fields and head more directly west. However, as the landscape becomes misty and unfamiliar, I begin to regret my decision. A dense fog surrounds me as I press onwards. Tall reeds rise up around me and midges flit through the air, conveying the sense that there is a body of water close by. Sure enough, I soon stumble upon the edge of a marsh. I narrowly avoid submersing my boot in the green-grey water. The rain has stopped, but the air is humid. Crickets chirp among the reeds. I trace my way around the edge of the marsh as best I can. My face is sticky with salty tears. My feet are cold and clammy in my boots. The wound on my arm has stopped weeping, but a thin red line remains.

I must look like an abysmal sight: tired, bloodied, puffy-eyed and damp all over.

Suddenly, the sound of crickets diminuendos, leaving an ominous silence. The temperature drops.

I'm not alone.

A figure stands shrouded in the mist ahead. I recognise her by her midnight blue cloak and veil: the Witch I saw in the village when I was a child. She stands watching me as if I was a snail on the wall, her head tilted ever-so-slightly to the side. For the second time today, I feel naked with my clothes on.

I keep walking towards her. I get the feeling I'm supposed to talk to her. An invisible string reels me in.

Finally, we stand face-to-face. I wait in silence while she looks me up and down.

She speaks. Her voice is deep. "You look like you're in a hurry."

"A pack of Twisteds is headed for Schlafhold," I explain. "Will you help us?"

"Help you? How would I do that?"

"I don't know, turn them into trees?"

The Witch squints at me. "I have no such powers. I am not a Forest Witch."

"Oh. Well then, what kind of Witch are you?"

She simply stares at me.

"So you won't help us?" I ask. I feel a ripple of anger pass through me.

"I have something for you," she says. "A gift."

I know better than to accept something from a Witch. "If you're not going to help the village, there is nothing you can give me. I want nothing."

"Your mother is ill."

I freeze. The Witch holds me in her gaze, unblinking.

Could she really heal Ma? My heart tells me she can. It's the kind of thing a Witch could do, when no-one else could.

"She will wake up tomorrow as if no affliction ever touched her," says the Witch. "She will return in all her beauty, all her joy."

I imagine sitting by Ma's side as she wakes up, her gaze narrowing in recognition before her face breaks into a wide smile. The feeling of her hand clasping mine. The look on Dad's face. The tears of relief he would cry. It makes my heart ache.

"At what cost?" I ask, my voice trembling.

The Witch smiles. "A small cost. Insignificant."

"Tell me."

"You carry something. A gift from a lover."

A gift from a lover? The only 'gift' I have from Cillian is a wound on my arm. And he probably doesn't count as a lover anymore. "I have no lover and carry nothing. Sorry to disappoint."

"A token of luck," says the Witch.

Luck? My hand drifts to the wooden horse in my pocket. The gift from... Haystack. Poor old Haystack, working hard at the stables all day long. Helping me with everything I ask. Always greeting me with a smile. Always so kind.

He did only lend it to me. But surely he wouldn't mind if I gave it away? I could tell him I lost it. He would forgive me.

But what did he say the last time I saw him? His horses were sick after a run of bad luck. If he doesn't get his good luck charm back, things could get worse. Haystack's life and livelihood depends on those stables.

And yet... I could have Ma back.

"The choice is yours," says the Witch.

It is my choice. And what kind of choice would I make? Who am I?

CHAPTER 24

"**N**o," I say at last. "I won't do it."

The Witch blinks once beneath her veil, perhaps a minute sign of annoyance.

The problem of the Twisteds remains. The Witch has made it evident that she is not going to help. Cillian has abandoned me. I'm all alone.

But maybe I am all I need. All that the village needs. Even if Cillian isn't here to say it, I'm still brave, and useful, and strong. I am capable of making a difference, even without Cillian by my side.

"I have to warn the village," I say, and step forwards.

The Witch narrows her eyes at me.

Suddenly, a familiar voice – a woman's voice – calls out from behind me.

"Minnow!" Raina's voice is strained, almost yelping. She pushes her way through the reeds.

I look back to the Witch, but she has disappeared. The marsh is suddenly alive again with noisy crickets and ribbiting frogs.

Raina's black hair has frizzed up in the humidity. She looks at me, wide-eyed, forehead wrinkled in concern.

"I've been looking for you," she puffs, breathless. "I had a bad feeling about Haunted Lake, so I came after you. I saw your footprints leave the track."

"Did you see any Twisteds?"

"Twisteds? No, why? Did you see another one at Haunted Lake? Wait, what happened to your arm?" She reaches out towards my injured arm, but I step away.

Raina frowns. "What's wrong?"

"Cillian told me. About you."

Raina's concerned expression turns to one of deep sadness. "I see." For a moment, in her crestfallen visage, I glimpse the lines of age and experience on her face. However, they soon vanish.

"Let me guess," I say. "It's like a game to you. Travelling to different villages, picking up girls, moving on before they can figure out your secret. You used me."

Raina shakes her head emphatically. "It's not like that. Not at all."

"So, what? You have real feelings for me?"

Raina squirms under my fierce gaze. "It's... more complicated than that."

"I must look so pathetic in your eyes. A child."

"No, Minnow. Please, just... Just listen for a moment."

I cross my arms and stare at her expectantly.

"I'm Cursed," she says. "I thought it was a Blessing. I stay youthful forever. Which, in itself, can feel like a Curse at times. But there's another catch. I can never fall in love."

"Never fall in love? As in, you'll never find the right partner?"

"No, as in, anyone I fall in love with will also be Cursed. I've seen it happen. I fell for a woman who lived in my neighbourhood, many years ago. I watched as she wasted away, her strength draining from her in a matter of weeks. My love is fatal."

"But why would you ever agree to a deal so horrible? Surely the idea of ageing wasn't that detestable to you?"

Raina sighs and shifts uncomfortably on the spot. "At the time I met the Witch, it suited me perfectly. I had given birth to Cillian's mother four months prior. I was the saddest I had ever been. In a real dark place. My husband had left me shortly after the birth. I believed he was disgusted by my body – the marks from the pregnancy, the constant weariness on my face in the weeks that followed. Given the pain of losing him, never falling in love again seemed like a desirable – even easy – option. And making myself beautiful forever would show him just how big a mistake he'd made." She looks down. "But it didn't take me long to realise that what I felt for him had never been true love. I wasn't built to love a man."

"What is it with your family and Curses?" I grumble, but immediately regret how heartless I sound. The truth is, I feel sorry for Raina.

"I liked you the moment I first saw you," Raina admits. "I never intended to take advantage. I mean, oh boy, you're naive – Cillian told me that long before I met you. But that wasn't why I wanted you. I liked *you*, because of who you are." She clears her throat. "If you want me to leave, I will. I understand that you feel betrayed. But really, underneath it all, I'm just a person. Just like you."

"Cillian told you I'm naive?"

Raina nods. "He said he could tell you anything and you'd believe it."

My insides tie up in knots. Cillian had preyed on my obliviousness all along. Again, I realise just how much of a mess I've made by choosing him over my own family.

Raina frowns. "Has he done something?"

I laugh bitterly. "Only stabbed me, broken my heart and abandoned me."

Raina's eyes bulge. "He did that to you?" She reaches out for my arm again. I don't draw away this time. She stares at the wound and shakes her head in confusion.

"But... why?" she whispers.

"He needed my blood for his Counterspell," I answer.

"Blood of the devoted," she murmurs.

"You knew about it?"

"I know it is an ingredient for some Spells. I didn't realise Cillian needed it. That makes sense. But... I can't believe he would treat you so cruelly. To think my own grandson..." Her voice trails away.

A distant screech reminds me why I am here. "We have to go."

The sight of Schlafhold's candlelit windows brings a sense of hope and relief. We cross the bridge and stand facing the main street.

"What now?" asks Raina.

"We need to tell everybody," I reply. "Start knocking on doors, I guess. I'll take the right side of town."

Raina runs off to the nearest house on the left. I look to the closest building on my right: Haystack's farmhouse.

I rap on the wooden door until my knuckles hurt.

Haystack opens it, bleary-eyed and dishevelled. "Minnow. Sorry, I decided to have an early night. What's wrong?"

I explain to him that a horde of Twisteds are on their way from Haunted Lake.

Haystack's eyes widen in horror. "Are you hurt? Oh my, you are!"

"I'm fine. But we need to alert the village. Oh, and before I forget..." I hold out the wooden horse.

Haystack takes it and holds it up between his thumb and index finger. "I would offer to let you keep it, but things have gone downhill without my lucky charm."

I smile. "It's back where it belongs."

We continue down the street knocking on doors, disturbing suppers, waking weary citizens, and causing a disruption unlike anything I've ever experienced in Schlafhold. Some villagers, like Everett and Sal, grab their protection knives and head towards the bridge. Others, like Prudence, hover outside their homes to watch what everyone else does. Poppy gathers her children into one room and starts barricading the front door.

Soon, a sizeable crowd has gathered by the bridge. Some hold lanterns or blazing torches to light up the night.

As Raina and I weave through the crowd, people hurl questions at us.

"How many Twisteds are there?"

"Why are they coming now?"

"When will they get here?"

Then, a familiar deep voice: "My daughter! Where is my daughter?"

I look up and see Dad pushing his way through the crowd, looking around desperately.

He sees me and beelines in my direction.

I take a deep breath and prepare to be berated. You shouldn't have gone to Haunted Lake, Minnow. You shouldn't have run off with some boy you hardly knew. You shouldn't have abandoned your family. Now look what you've done.

Dad says none of these things. Instead, he scoops me into a warm hug. His stubble scratches against my forehead.

"Thank you for coming back," he whispers.

"I should never have left," I reply.

"You did what you needed to do. You're old enough to make your own choices and have a life of your own. It's my fault I pushed you away. The thought of losing you..." His voice trails away.

I shake my head. "I lost sight of what's important. You. Ma. The bakery. The village."

Raina claps her hands to get everyone's attention. I scan the crowd and see Betty standing nearby, a confused look cemented on her face. Cillian is nowhere in sight. I guess he really did leave already.

"A group of Twisteds from the forest beyond Haunted Lake is headed this way," Raina explains. "They'll be here any minute. There's no time to leave. We have to defend the village."

Alarmed murmurs spread among the crowd. As far as I know, Everett is the only person with any kind of combat experience. Beyond very basic training, protection knives are only used for customary greetings.

We can't win this fight.

So, maybe it doesn't have to be a fight. We have to stop the Twisteds from reaching the village at all.

"The bridge," I murmur. Then, I speak up. "We have to destroy the bridge. If the bridge is broken, the Twisteds won't be able to get across the river and into the village."

"But we just built that bridge," argues Prudence indignantly, clearly not grasping the seriousness of the threat.

Bickering breaks out. I feel the tension in my shoulders increasing as I realise that while we're arguing, the Twisteds are drawing ever nearer. In fact, I can see their silhouettes on the horizon. At least twenty, maybe more.

Everett raises his beefy hand to silence the crowd. Even without speaking, his presence commands respect. "I don't think we should destroy the bridge. If they come this way, the Twisteds will all be funnelled into the space of the bridge and we can take them out as they cross."

No-one else has noticed the Twisteds approaching in the distance yet. If they had, they would realise there was no way we could defeat them all.

Then, a thought occurs to me. Mugwort. The herb that repels Twisteds.

I look to my left and see Heron standing a few metres away. I go over to her and tug on her sleeve to get her attention.

"What is it, Minnow?"

"How much mugwort do you have?" I ask.

Heron's brow creases in confusion. Then, her eyes widen as she understands what I am thinking. "Mugwort... I received a crate from Harethorn about a month ago. I've used a little... but there is at least half a box left."

"It would buy us some time," I say.

Heron nods and hurries towards the apothecary.

"Listen!" I call out, grabbing the villagers' attention. "We need to build a fire and keep it burning. The smell of burning mugwort will keep the Twisteds away."

"That's just part of the old folklore," white-haired Mr Gust pipes up. "There's no saying it will actually work."

"We have to try," I urge.

A scream erupts as Prudence spots the approaching Twisteds lumbering towards the bridge. Mere minutes away.

Some villagers rush to grab firewood and start stacking it on the close end of the bridge, blocking the way across.

Heron hurries back up the street, carrying a crate full of bundles of mugwort. I give her a hand and we place the crate by the logs of firewood. Haystack starts the fire.

I turn back to Dad. "Is Ma safe?"

"Yes. And her fever's gone." He pauses. Then, "She loves you, you know. I know she would appreciate everything you've done to try and help her. I appreciate it... even if I don't always show it. I heard about what you did to save Cillian's cousin, too. I'm proud of you, Minnow. And I missed you while you were gone."

"I'm glad to be back," I say. "Back with you and Ma."

Dad squeezes my hand. Then, he reaches into his apron pocket and pulls out something wrapped in paper. "I saved you half a loaf. It's fresh."

I hold the bread up to my nose and inhale the scent. It smells like home.

"I was thinking..." I say, "I'm not sure I want to keep working at the bakery. At least, not all the time."

"Oh?" Dad looks curious, but not disappointed.

"I think the wider world needs me. And I need the wider world."

"The wider world is lucky to have you."

Amidst the chaos and terror, I feel a sense of peace. Despite the threat, my village is here. The people are with me. The people who have guided and protected me my whole life. It doesn't matter that I don't have Cillian. I have Schlafhold. I have my family. I'm not the same person I was a few weeks ago, and yet I'm more myself than ever.

Stacie Turner is an Australian author based in Canberra (Ngunnawal Country). Stacie has a passion for writing about fantastical worlds and the unusual creatures inhabiting them. When not writing, Stacie enjoys fishkeeping, hiking, and drawing inspiration from nature.